I0624804

CUT TO THE CHASE

SUTTON CAPITAL INTRIGUE SERIES BOOK 3

LORI RYAN

ALSO BY LORI RYAN

The Sutton Capital Series

Legal Ease

Penalty Clause

The Baker's Bodyguard (A Sutton Capital Series Novella)

Negotiation Tactics

The Billionaire's Suite Dreams

The Baker, the Bodyguard, and the Wedding Bell Blues (A
Sutton Capital Series Novella)

Her SEALed Fate

The Sutton Capital Series Boxed Set (Books One Through Four)

The Sutton Capital Series Boxed Set (Books Five Through
Seven)

Sutton Capital Intrigue

Cutthroat

Cut and Run

Cut to the Chase

Sutton Capital On the Line Series

Pure Vengeance

Latent Danger

Wicked Justice

Heroes of Evers, Texas Series

Love and Protect

Promise and Protect

Honor and Protect (An Evers, TX Novella)

Serve and Protect

Desire and Protect

Cherish and Protect

Triple Play Curse Series

Game Changer

Game Maker

Game Clincher

The Triple Play Curse Boxed Set

Standalone Books

Stealing Home (writing in Melanie Shawn's Hope Falls Series)

Any Witch Way (writing in Robyn Peterman's Magic and Mayhem Series)

All In (writing in the Sleeper SEALs Series)

ISBN: 978-1-941149-64-5

ACKNOWLEDGMENTS

There wouldn't be a book without Melanie and Steve having my back on this editing thing. Editing doesn't even begin to describe their contribution. Thank you, guys!

I'd also like to thank Lyman Connor of http://bionichandproject.com/ for his invaluable help in answering questions and sharing his expertise with me. The worm gear was perfect! Check out his website and story—you'll be glad you did! http://bionichandproject.com/

I'm sure Scott Silverii, Ph.D., must have answered at least one question for this book, and more than likely, it was a lot more than that. Probably twenty or so. Thank you for always answering the call! You amaze me.

I'd also like to thank Susan Thompson and Kelly Hill from the Yale Collection of Musical Instruments for taking the time to answer my questions. It's the little details that bring a story to life! I had so much fun poking around on the website. Take a look at that one, too, my reader friends! http://collection.yale.edu/instruments/keyboards/

None of my books would happen without the incredible

support of my husband and children. As always, a million thank you's to them!

Thank you to Ehlane for pulling it all together and to Kate and Kay for being there to listen and chug coffee! I love you guys.

CHAPTER 1

MOST PEOPLE WOULD SAY Warrick Staunton stayed in the house so long to punish himself. His penance.

They'd probably be right. Though the house and its grounds were gorgeous, he hadn't felt at home here in a long time. Every piece of artwork, every scrap of polished custom-designed furniture, every square foot carried ghosts.

"We're almost finished on the first floor, Mr. Staunton."

Warrick turned toward the voice and found one of the moving men standing in the doorway of the kitchen. The man shifted on his feet, as though he hoped Warrick wouldn't want to chat. He needn't worry. Warrick didn't.

He should have let Charlotte handle all of this. He should be at the office instead of watching them empty the house.

"Fine." He nodded and moved to the French doors overlooking the patio. The flagstones blended neatly into the lawn, with a small path leading the way to Vicki's rose garden. He looked to the one rose bush that sat apart from the rest. He'd have to come back for it after the movers left.

When the yard and house were quiet and he could dig it up in peace.

"I'm heading into the office, but Charlotte is here if you need anything." He needed to get out of here before it got any harder to breathe.

His assistant chose that moment to walk in. Her no-nonsense air drew the worker's attention and Warrick gladly relinquished control of the move to her. Charlotte was one of those assistants who no longer needed to be told what to do or what was a priority. She could all but run his life without him.

"Are you on track to be out of here by four?" she asked, earning a "yes ma'am" in response from the man.

"Good." She bobbed her head, making the short gray curls bounce. "I've got the cleaning crew coming in early this evening, so you'll have an hour or two buffer in there." Now she was speaking mostly to Warrick. "We're on schedule for the walk-through before the closing tomorrow morning."

Warrick slipped out as she and the mover spoke. Charlotte would take care of things while he focused on saving his company. He looked at his watch. He'd have just enough time to get there to meet with Jack Sutton and his group. He hoped like hell he was doing the right thing.

Warrick scrubbed at the back of his neck as he walked out to his car and tossed his wallet and keys on the center console. Simms Pharmaceutical had been in his family for generations. His great grandfather had started the company and it had always been privately held by his family members.

Now Warrick was on the verge of losing it. He didn't have any choice but to let Sutton Capital buy in, and hoped like hell all he'd heard about Jack Sutton was right. He was letting Sutton Capital buy an eighteen percent interest in the company. It wasn't a controlling interest, but since no one outside his family had ever owned any interest, it was significant. It would also mean the trust that held his and his mother's shares no longer held a majority. If he needed a majority vote on something now, his uncle would have to stand with him.

There was a time when Warrick would have been sure his uncle would always be by his side. That wasn't a given any more.

He maneuvered through the streets without hitting traffic, not something he normally got to do. Then again, he never went to the office this late. He slid his car into the spot reserved for him and walked toward the building, glancing at the park across the street. In another hour, the walking path he'd had put in for his employees would have people on it, making the lap during their lunch breaks in sneakers they'd swap out for work shoes. A few hours after that, there would be kids and moms at the playground in the park.

Life was moving on for most. For him, it seemed to be crumbling apart. Again. He honestly wasn't sure how many times he could put the pieces back together, but he'd do it once more, at least. He had to. There were a lot of people employed at his company. In the initial aftermath of the scandal, he'd wondered if he should step aside and let someone else try to rebuild.

None of his cousins were prepared to run the company, but they'd been outspoken about wanting someone else to do it. He knew, if given half the chance, they'd hire someone from the outside. He cringed at the thought of who they might choose. They had no concern for things like loyalty to their employees. When he'd put in childcare, they'd balked and called it a luxury that was coming out of their pockets.

Ultimately, he'd decided against making it easy for them. Simms Pharmaceutical had been started by his mother's grandfather. It was his responsibility to make sure the company didn't fail. When he was finished, he'd choose someone suitable to take his role and then—well, then he'd figure out what to do from there. He had a feeling he was finished here, though. Maybe he'd sell out after and move someplace quiet. Start something else.

Or retire. The thought boggled his mind. He was only thirty-five years old. What would he do? Play golf in Florida for the rest of his life? Not likely. He wasn't the kind of guy to sit around, but a remote cabin in the woods off the grid held a certain amount of appeal. Maybe he could find some new project he could work on remotely so he could take himself out of the world for a while.

He looked up at the Simms name etched in the glass front of the modern building. At least he'd been able to keep all the employees on to date. He knew they were wondering if they'd show up to closed doors one morning. He hoped like hell that never came to pass.

Warrick nodded at people as he made his way through the lobby and took the elevator up to the third floor on the administrative side of the building. The labs, research, and development side of the building was larger, housing five stories rather than three. The building was only a few years old. They'd moved to this space four years before, when things had been flush. Before all the trouble.

Warrick came up short in the employee kitchen, when faced with a woman he didn't recognize. He knew all the people that worked for him. Of course, it was possible she was a temp secretary—or she could be one of Jack's people. Sutton's team should be in the building shortly, but maybe they'd gotten here earlier than he'd thought they would.

As he watched, she went on tip-toes, arm outstretched to reach for a coffee mug. Most of his staff must already have needed a couple of rounds of caffeine. The lower shelf was empty of mugs, and only a few remained on the upper. She came down without a mug in hand. As he watched, he realized she wasn't reaching with her hand. She'd reached with the prosthesis attached to her hand. And, now, she made a couple of moves and extended the prosthesis with what looked like a telescoping effect of some sort, giving herself another two inches or so.

This time, when she reached, she grasped the mug and brought it down slowly. He heard her gasp as the mug slipped when it was within inches of the counter. It fell with a loud clunk but didn't break.

"Go-go gadget," he said, then realized that might be offensive. It had just been what came to mind when he saw her prosthesis. He wanted to see more of it. See what it could do. He wondered who had developed it. It wasn't anything he'd heard of out in the market. Of course, Simms wasn't involved in prosthetics or devices, so he didn't keep tabs on that side of things the way he did the pharmaceutical side, but he was fascinated by what he'd just seen.

She spun, surprise in her eyes, and he realized she hadn't known he was there. Great. He'd offended *and* startled her.

"I'm sorry. I didn't mean—"

She watched him for a minute, then put the coffee mug down and slipped past him without a word.

"Okay," he said to the empty room, moving forward to fill the mug she'd left behind. He grabbed another off the shelf and filled it for himself, then followed her out and down the hall. As he'd thought, she went into the office he'd set up as a temporary work area for Jack Sutton's group. It was a small conference room. Warrick's office manager had arranged three desks on one side, and a small table and chairs on the other, giving them plenty of room to settle in when they were here.

"Morning, Jack." He nodded at Jack Sutton, then put the coffee in front of the woman.

"Warrick." Jack rose to shake his hand, then gestured to the woman. "This is Sara Blackburn. She handles anything we take on having to do with electronics, electromagnetics, that kind of thing."

"Yeah," Sara said, standing now. It almost seemed as though it pained her to ask the question, and Warrick had the feeling questioning chain-of-command was hard on her. She did it anyway. "I'm not sure why you wanted me here, Jack. I mean, I've looked over the company," she carefully avoided looking Warrick's way, "and they don't make any medical devices. There's no engineering or electronics or anything here. I don't think I can be of help on this project."

CHAPTER 2

SARA EYED THE TWO MEN. Warrick had startled her in the employee kitchen, and that in and of itself left her shaken. No one snuck up on her. She heard everyone coming. It was a side effect from her time in the military, and it had stuck, just as it did for a lot of combat veterans. She was aware of her surroundings. Plain and simple.

Only, she hadn't been when he'd walked in. She'd been focused on getting out of this project. She had planned to talk to Jack in advance, but he'd been on the phone since she got in this morning. Now she was stuck trying to talk her way out of this project with the CEO in the same room with them.

Still, would she have come right out and told Jack why she didn't want to be involved with Simms Pharmaceutical either way? Maybe. Jack was an understanding man. He might get where she was coming from. But how do you say I can't work for these people because they're killers and the thought of being involved with them makes my stomach churn?

She'd been lucky in her work at Sutton Capital so far. Jack Sutton didn't choose to work with companies that didn't seem to have some ethical standards to them. Until now, that is.

Most of the companies Sutton Capital financed were small startups or mom and pop types of places, where she'd felt she was giving the little guys a way to make their dreams work.

But how do you say "you're backing a heartless killer" to your boss?

She understood that Simms Pharmaceutical wasn't responsible for what a madman had done with their drug. The news reports had made that clear. It was William Tyvek who'd taken a failed drug from Simms Pharmaceutical and used it to kill a dozen or more homeless men, many of them veterans like herself. But she'd dug deeper. She knew the drug Tyvek had used had been cancelled after it had killed several people in a Simms Pharmaceutical drug trial. And Simms Pharmaceutical had paid off the families and walked away, washing their hands of it all.

Lives were wrecked, and they'd simply walked away as if nothing could touch them. And now here was Warrick Staunton, a guy born with a silver spoon in his mouth if she ever saw one, standing here like the world owed him something.

The world didn't owe this guy anything.

Sara didn't look at him. She kept her gaze on Jack, wondering if she could use some kind of mind meld to impress upon him how much she didn't want to be here. Surely if she could explain her position to him, he could just as easily assign one of the other members of the tech team to this deal.

To her surprise, she saw Jack grin as though he didn't

care at all that she would question him in front of someone else. "I have you here because I think you can help us save Simms Pharmaceutical. Simple as that, Sara."

"I don't understand," she said slowly. Typically, when she came to something like this with Jack, her job was to analyze the technology and assess the costs and benefits associated with each area of a company's business. Then she'd make suggestions for where the company could or should make cuts, improvements and so forth.

From what she'd heard, Simms would need to make a lot of cuts, starting with laying off over half of its workforce. Warrick Staunton and his head researcher, Jonathan Simms, of course were safe. They were family, and essentially owned the company other than the portion of it that Jack had just bought, and the very small percentages owned by a number of cousins.

"You think outside the box. You always have. Both at work and with the work you and Samantha have been doing on your prostheses. I want that kind of thinking for this." Now Jack's look included both Sara and Warrick. "I don't think fixing Simms is going to be a matter of continuing to do what's always been done. Just cutting staff or cutting product lines isn't going to fix the issue here."

"I won't cut staff unless I absolutely have to," Warrick said. "I won't be taking a salary this year, or next if need be. I've got enough money to keep the staff on for at least six months even if sales stay stagnant."

Sara was impressed, but wondered how he planned to do that. The employees wouldn't have anything to make. Orders for the company's business had fallen off dramatically.

Sure, there were a few medications where they held the patent and there was no generic equivalent or competitor making a replacement. Orders for those drugs hadn't been hurt. But where there was a replacement option? Well, it seemed some doctors were choosing to shift patients to those options. Either that or the patients had asked to be switched. Bad publicity could hurt anyone nowadays.

Warrick echoed what she'd just thought. "They won't have much to do, but I've found enough money to keep them on."

How do you *find* enough money to keep a full sales force, the scientists and lab technicians, the support staff, on? Was he that rich that he had piles sitting around in a closet he'd forgotten all about? Hell, she'd be psyched to find twenty bucks she'd forgotten about in a winter coat. Had this guy found a random extra few million in a coat pocket? She almost laughed at the image she'd lodged in her head, but stifled it in time.

"All right, so let's come up with a plan that's going to get the company out of this."

Sara sat down and closed her mouth. She had to admit, hearing Jack say he had that kind of confidence in her floored her. And felt good. Maybe she was shortchanging Warrick and Simms. If Jack believed in them enough to be here, that said a lot about them, and one thing Sara had learned in the military was to be open to the opinions of those around her. Listening to your teammates can save your ass overseas.

She blew out a breath. "All right. Well, the obvious thing would be a PR campaign, but we don't really want obvious here." The men waited and Sara kept going. It was how she brainstormed. She talked through problems until she came up with a solution. Of course, she usually did this in her office with the door closed and only proposed the end result to other people. Having the men watch and listen while she talked was unnerving.

"Your employees need something to do in the meantime. We can't train them to be PR gurus overnight." She chewed on her lower lip and looked out the window, talking almost under her breath now. "But they could learn to do something else overnight maybe. They're scientists and lab technicians. Some of them can be researching new drugs if there's funding for that. It's really the production and sales force we need to repurpose."

She stopped for a minute and watched people walking through the park across the street. Warrick had an enormous floor to ceiling wall of windows that looked out on a green vista of trees and walking paths with benches. Off to one side of the park was a small playground with a slide and swings.

"The ideal solution would be a project your current staff can work on but that also provides the PR solution. A project that *is* the PR solution." She still didn't know what the heck that was, and she hoped Jack got that she was just spouting every thought that came to her for the moment. Surely, he wouldn't expect her to come up with the answer right here and now. She turned in her chair to tell Jack she needed some time to work on this alone, but found him pointing at her with a wide smile on his face.

"What?"

"You're brilliant." He didn't explain the statement. Just leaned forward in his chair. "Do you have your prosthetic hand proposal on your laptop?"

It took a few seconds but she saw where he was headed and she wasn't sure if she liked it or not. If she was honest, he was right. It was exactly what they needed. And in reality, it would be exactly what she'd been looking for as well.

It was almost embarrassing she hadn't seen it herself before he did. That didn't change the fact that she felt nervous showing her proposal to Warrick Staunton, and she wasn't at all sure she wanted the poster girl for saving Simms to be *her*.

"You know it's perfect." Jack was still smiling at her.

"Okay, care to share with the class?" Warrick said, looking between Jack and Sara.

Jack smiled. "If Sara okays it, you're going to be making her prosthetic hands. And you're going to be giving them away to veterans in need. It will mean hiring a few new employees, which will also be good for PR. We'll also redirect some of the current employees there, but obviously not all of them will find a skill set that matches the new project. For them, we need to get orders up within the next six months, but this gives us a little time and a hell of a PR strategy to bring people back around to the company."

He recapped exactly what Sara had been looking for in a company sponsor for her prostheses. Samantha, her friend and co-worker at Sutton, had helped her put all the pieces of the proposal together, but none of the companies she'd approached had bought into it yet. They all wanted her technology, of course. But none of them liked her conditions.

She wanted a company to cap the amount charged to those who could pay for her devices, and to give a portion of the product to veterans at no charge. A pipe dream, it turned out. No company who had the funding to produce the devices on a larger scale than she could was willing to give up a damned thing, despite the fact she was asking pennies for the technology itself.

The problem for Sara was that she had no interest in making money. Companies, on the other hand, did. They wouldn't mind writing her a check for ten times the money she wanted for the technology. She'd started her prosthesis using known tech that was out there for the taking, but in the process, she'd innovated a few of the pieces related to grasp strength and biomimicry. She had considered simply putting the specs out there for everyone to see and use online. The only problem was, the average person couldn't do anything with that.

What she wanted was for a company with the equipment and funding to make it on a larger scale, make some money—a reasonable, fair amount of money—making it, but also have the project be partially charitable. She might as well be looking for a ride on a paper airplane to Mars.

She pulled up the proposal on her laptop and put it in front of Warrick. Samantha had run numbers, and created projections and charts, and put it all together in a gorgeous package. That didn't mean she wanted Warrick Staunton looking at her baby. He wasn't nearly as approachable as Jack was. He seemed all business and her stomach tightened as he scanned the data she and Samantha had compiled. He looked up at Jack after a few moments. "You've checked all of this? It can be done?"

Jack nodded. He had reviewed the project for her and had told her he'd keep an eye out for companies that might be a good match and more open to her idea. "Yes. It's all accurate. The deal Sara would be giving the company would be a steal. You'd have to agree to the terms she's laid out. The PR Simms Pharmaceutical would get from the donated prostheses will give us our best shot at recovery in the market. With any luck, that should drive your sales back up. Down the road someday, you'll also make a nice profit, but in the short term, the goal is simply to build goodwill."

Warrick was silent a moment and Sara sought the words

to voice her objection. What was her objection? What did she have to complain about? Jack was handing her everything she'd asked for. She couldn't ask for better than this.

Then her problem opened his mouth and spoke, and she realized it was Warrick Staunton who was bothering her. The thought of being his way out, the way to save his company, somehow disgusted her.

Warrick looked at the prosthesis she wore on her arm now. She was still wearing the prototype she'd been messing with earlier. It wasn't ready for anyone to see it in action. She hadn't gotten the grip strength to work reliably and there were problems with some of the digits bending properly. She moved her arm to the side. Warrick showed her a page from the file Jack had handed him. The prosthesis she and Samantha had designed was on the page, laid out with specifications and details in the side margins of the page.

"This doesn't look like that." Warrick frowned as he nodded to the prosthesis on her computer screen.

"It's not," Sara said simply, then stood crossing to the other side of the room. She turned her back and opened her bag to remove the prosthesis she wore most days. The robotic one he'd seen in the proposal with all the bells and whistles.

She and Samantha often messed around with other ideas. They'd created a prosthesis that had changeable gadgets to fit in a standardized base. The gadgets were customized for the user's purpose. So, a person could fit it with a knife for cooking or a hammer if they worked in construction. They were fun and handy, but they also had to switch the tool with each use.

The benefit to the robotic hand she took out of the bag now was that it allowed the user to grip tools with the hand itself, much in the way someone with a natural hand might.

As much as she loved playing around with the tooled prostheses she and Samantha were making, they had a lot of downsides to them. So did a standard prosthesis. Rather than your typical prosthesis which had "open" or "close" as the only two options, the bionic hand she now fit to her stump allowed for a variety of finger movements and grips. It worked by feeling movements she made with the muscles of her arm and responded accordingly to shift and adjust the pressure and grip type.

There were others like it on the market, but nothing that compared as far as cost to bring to market. That had been her main focus during the design process. To come up with a bionic hand that had the features it needed; the materials to withstand wear, tear, and time; and cost effective production. Most bionic hands were out of reach of the average consumer because of their price.

It took her a few moments to change the prosthesis. She crossed back to the men when she'd finished. This hand had the shape of a natural hand, but the material was purple in color. She could have chosen a plain white or even tan, but her hand would never look completely natural, so she'd given up on not drawing attention to herself. People would look. Let them.

Where the digits of the fingers connected to the hand, there were rings of metal visible through the rubber. Two electrodes on the inside of the socket rested against the two muscles on her arm. The hand moved in response to small movements of those muscles. The hand looked surprisingly nimble as she flexed the fingers. She knew it wasn't what most people expected.

She watched as Warrick glanced back at the page, then to her hand, then back again a few times. He nodded. "Done. Thanks, Jack."

That was it. He walked out.

Sara looked at Jack, back to the door Warrick Staunton had just walked through, and back to Jack. Then back to the door. She could go on all day like this and still not have words for the rudeness of the man who'd just exited.

CHAPTER 3

WILLIAM TYVEK WATCHED from a distance as the house was emptied bit by bit. He fumed at Warrick, but really, he knew he had himself to blame for much of what was happening now. He'd somehow messed this all up. His plan had been perfect. He had set everything up from the start to take Warrick Staunton to his knees. To take everything away from the man who'd taken William's daughter from him. The fact that Warrick had walked away unscathed was yet another example of the way nothing stuck to Warrick Staunton.

William had done everything right, set up every detail to point to Warrick Staunton as the mastermind behind illegal drug testing that was killing New Haven's homeless men. He'd used leverage to pull in just the right people to point the finger at Warrick. The police had still somehow gone looking elsewhere. Warrick Staunton seemed immune and that had to stop.

A flash of red caught his eye and William turned as his heart sped up.

It was her. It had to be. His Vicki had come back.

He glanced back at the house but didn't see anyone around. The men must all be inside now, wrapping up the final pieces of furniture for moving. He sped up, moving toward the garden at the back of the house. It was her favorite spot.

He caught sight of the little girl in her bright red dress once more. He knew the dress. Her nanny had bought it for her for Christmas one year but she'd worn it well into the summer, despite its heavy velour fabric. She'd loved that dress and the way it swished around her knees when she spun in a circle.

She turned now, and he caught sight of cheeks reddened from the cold and a laughing smile, but when she spotted him, she ran.

William followed, but knew he wouldn't catch her.

His daughter ran from him whenever he saw her now. It had started the day he'd taken Carrie Hastings and tried to frame Warrick for her death. That had been a mistake. A mistake that had turned Victoria against him. He'd been trying to find his way back to her since then.

"Hey! You can't be back here!"

The shout came from behind him, but William didn't bother to turn. He walked further into the wooded area behind the garden and yard. He knew how to cut through the woods and disappear before anyone could catch up to him. It was harder now with his leg the way it was. Moving hadn't been as easy for him lately. But the person yelling was at the house. It would take them time to catch up to him, and most likely, they wouldn't bother.

This was the last time he'd be back to the house. Victoria was gone. She'd left him, and he supposed he couldn't blame her. He'd screwed up everything.

* * *

"So, the problem is?" Samantha drew out the question, using tone more than anything to tell Sara she was being unreasonable. Sara didn't need her best friend to tell her that. She was well aware.

"I guess I just don't like the idea of being this guy's bailout." Sara paused as the baby began to stir in his car seat. Samantha reached a hand over casually and rocked the car seat where it sat on a chair next to them, picking up her coffee and sipping it as she did. It never ceased to amaze Sara how easily and quickly Samantha had taken to motherhood.

Joey was so tiny, and only three months old. Sara only held him occasionally, still worried she would break him, or worse, drop him. And the fear had nothing to do with her prosthetic hand. She would have that fear regardless. She didn't understand how women went from not knowing what in the world they were doing to skilled mommies who could juggle a newborn, pretty much overnight.

"It's the best of both worlds." Samantha shook her head at Sara, her brow furrowed. "You get what you need, he gets what he needs."

Before Sara could reply, they were joined by Jill and Jennie. All but Jill worked at Sutton Capital together. Samantha was married to Logan, who also used to work at Sutton Capital. Jennie was married to Chad, Jack's cousin and head of security at Sutton Capital. Jill was the only one of them who didn't work at Sutton. She was a photographer, but her husband, Andrew, was the chief financial officer at Sutton, and also Chad and Jack's best friend.

Jill and Jennie spent a few minutes cooing over baby Joey before Jennie turned a mischievous grin on Sara. "Are we talking about Warrick Staunton? Because if that man has needs, you should think about taking care of them." Jennie added an eyebrow waggle to emphasize her point.

Sara laughed, shaking her head. She'd never been able to manage waggling her eyebrows like that. "I'm not going to be taking care of any of his needs. I don't like the man."

"What's not to like?" Jill shared a look with Jennie and Samantha and the girls all laughed. Sara understood. Warrick Staunton was easily one of the best-looking men she'd ever met. But he was too good-looking. He had that look of somebody who could have walked out of the pages of a magazine. Not someone who actually existed in the real world, or ever lifted a finger for anything. Not her type. Not even remotely.

"He's like a moody Simon Baker." Jennie said.

"No," Jill shook her head. "Bradley Cooper."

The three women sighed in unison, but Sara laughed, ignoring the fact that Jill was pretty spot on. "Sorry, I like my men a little more down to earth than that guy."

"I think he's kind of perfect. He's the perfect combination," Samantha said.

"Combination?" Jennie asked, ignoring Sara's eye roll.

"Sure," Samantha grinned. "He's sort of cold and closed off, but he's super hot at the same time. So, no entanglements. He's too aloof for that. But I bet you anything he's as hot as he looks in bed."

Sara had a feeling he wasn't as aloof as people thought he was, but she didn't voice that. No, she needed to sidetrack Samantha. "Shouldn't your mind be on your husband? You know, the father of your baby, love of your life?" Sara challenged.

Samantha laughed. "Oh trust me, my mind's on Logan. I just think *your* mind should be on Warrick Staunton."

Sara didn't have a chance to voice the *ha!* that echoed in her head as she looked at her friend and tried to decide just how serious Samantha was.

"I don't know," Jill said, "he's got that brooding, I'm-a-man-in-need-of-healing thing going on. It's kind of sexy. Would you like to help him heal?"

Sara groaned. "No. That's the last thing I need. Now can we drop this and talk about what really matters?"

She saw the look between the three women but ignored it. She really meant what she said. The last thing she needed in her life was a man. The last one walked out on her while she was still recovering in the hospital.

Samantha nodded with an over serious look on her face. "You got it. So we're talking about your prosthesis right?"

"Yes." Sara hoped the other women would move off topic with Samantha.

"What about it? Did you find a buyer?" Jennie sat forward as she asked. They all knew she'd been looking for a long time for somebody to work with her on her prosthetics project.

"The brooding hottie is going to make them." So much for Samantha helping Sara to change the topic.

"No kidding? So you'll be seeing a lot of broody boy?" Jennie frowned. "We really need to figure out a better nickname for him."

"No, we really don't." Sara needed to nip this in the bud before it became a thing. She'd seen what happened when things became a thing with this group. This was clearly becoming a thing.

"I know, it's great, right?" Samantha lifted a now fussy Joey out of his car seat and settled him over one shoulder. She somehow held him in place with the left hand while she reached under her shirt with the right hand. Seconds later, she had him tucked in there nursing away. "We weren't getting anywhere with finding a company to produce the prosthetics the way that Sara wanted them to be produced, with the donations and everything. So, we took it to Jack and asked him for help."

Sara grumbled. "If I'd known this was the kind of help he would give..."

"Oh stop," Samantha said. "This is going to be great, and you know it."

"Time out. Back it up for those of us who have no idea what's going on." Jill waived a hand as she spoke.

Samantha didn't give Sara time to answer. She jumped right in to answer for her. "Sara's prostheses have been ready to go for a long time. But it turns out, she can't produce enough of them on her own to make it worthwhile. She's got a far-greater list of veterans wanting one than she can handle. So we've been searching for a company to buy the technology. She would give them an overly-generous deal and, in exchange, she wanted them to give a certain percentage of the product away free, and another percentage away at a large discount."

"And no one will do that?" Jill asked, looking to Sara.

"No." Sara polished off the coffee cake she hadn't needed but couldn't resist. She'd lost the lean muscled build she'd had over in Iraq. She wasn't overweight, but she was softer now.

"But now broody boy says he will," Samantha said with a grin.

Jennie laughed. "Sorry, Sara. The name is stuck."

"Ugh."

"Okay, but seriously," Jill said. "What's your objection to Warrick Staunton's company doing this?"

Three pairs of eyes stared back at her. Well, four, if you

counted baby Joey, who was taking a break from his nursing and now seemed to watch her almost as intently as the other women.

Sara opened her mouth, then closed it again. She didn't know how to articulate her objection. She tried anyway. "I guess I just feel like this guy's not doing it for the right reasons. I mean, his company just needs the publicity. I wanted someone to do it because they cared about veterans, not because he needs a gimp for a poster child."

"Sara!" Jill said.

Sara shrugged. "Sorry, but, it's true. He's just using me."

The group was quiet for a minute, but Samantha spoke up. "It sounds like you'll be saving his employees' jobs. He'll also be hiring new people, so that's good, too."

Sara nodded. "You're right." She felt a little like a petulant child who'd been corrected. "He did say he had enough money to keep his employees on for six months. Jack thinks if we can change the company's image, that will be enough to save them. There are some medications they have patents on that doctors won't ever stop prescribing, so they have somewhat of a cushion, regardless of how the public views them. It's the things doctors don't need to prescribe that are the issue."

Samantha leaned in and spoke quietly, so only the group could hear. "I overheard Jack and Chad talking this morning. Jack said Warrick sold his home to keep the employees on. He's moving into a townhouse."

"Wow." Jennie's brows went up. "That's gotta mean something. Maybe he's not just a cold-hearted corporate dick-head, after all."

Jill laughed. "Let's hope not. Broody boy is a lot easier to say than cold-hearted dick-head corporate ass guy."

CHAPTER 4

WARRICK REVIEWED THE NUMBERS AGAIN. Jack was right. They could make this work. When it came down to it, the prescription side of things wasn't suffering all that much. The over-the-counter medications were another story. It didn't matter in the mind of consumers that his company hadn't actually been the one to test the drug on homeless people. All that mattered was that they'd been linked to the story and people remembered the name Simms with homeless people being killed. It was enough. Stock prices were down nearly thirty percent, and the free fall didn't seem set to end anytime soon.

He looked out the window at the park across the street from his office and recognized Sara Blackwell immediately. Her bulky coat didn't cover her no-nonsense walk. She seemed to always have a purpose, direction. She walked as if she had a place to be and a job to do, and he found himself liking that about her. She might not like him—that much had been clear when they'd met yesterday, although he had no idea why. He liked her. She didn't seem fragile or needy.

She'd spoken her mind with Jack. That said a lot about her character.

As he watched, she approached one of the few homeless people currently taking up residence in the park. Connecticut was on the verge of eradicating chronic homelessness in the state, but that didn't mean there weren't still transients filling the spots on the benches in some of the parks. Sara produced a small bag, gave it to him, and said a few words to the man, before continuing to walk. The man's eyes followed her before he opened the bag and pulled something out. They were too far away for Warrick to see what it was, or much about either of them, but Sara kept walking like it was nothing. Simply part of her day to care for others.

"Mr. Staunton, I've got the papers for your signature from Mr. Carmichael's firm." Charlotte placed a cup of coffee and the *Financial Times* and *Wall Street Journal* on his desk as she spoke.

Carmichael Engineering would handle transforming one of the old burned out labs on their other property into a manufacturing facility for the prosthetic hands they'd be producing. Jack had already talked to them before bringing the idea to Warrick so all that was left was for Warrick to sign off on the plans for the space. Jack was paying a premium to have the facility finished in record time, and in the meantime, Warrick and his team would start on the press releases and PR effort.

His assistant slipped the few papers he'd stacked in his outbox into her arms and looked expectantly at him. "And Detective Harmon is here to see you."

Warrick nodded. "Send him in." He didn't have time to meet with anyone right now, but Jarrod Harmon wasn't just anyone.

The detective walked in moments after Charlotte left the room. Warrick stood and shook his hand, then waved for the detective to take a seat across from him. Many people might think it odd that he and Detective Harmon had become good friends. The man's investigation had derailed his company to the point that he may very well lose it all. It wasn't Harmon's fault and, in fact, the man had seen through the setup Tyvek had tried to build. He'd exposed the true man behind the horrific crime committed for, it seemed, no other purpose than to frame Warrick.

Not to mention Harmon had saved one of Warrick's oldest friends, Carrie Hastings, and the two were now dating.

"How's Carrie doing?" Warrick asked. He hadn't talked to her in a few weeks. Truth be told, it was hard to look her in the eye, knowing his failures had been at the heart of all of this. Months ago, Warrick had had regrets. Now, he didn't even know how to describe the depths of what he felt. William Tyvek might be the man behind the deaths of an untold number of homeless people, the very people Carrie had dedicated her life to helping, but when it came down to it, Warrick was the one who'd put it all into motion.

It was then that Warrick noticed how drawn and tired Jarrod's face was. When Tyvek took Carrie, he'd trapped her in a burning building, intending it to look like Warrick had killed her. Jarrod had saved her in time, but the fire had been started with chemicals. Between the smoke damage and the chemical inhalation, she'd suffered serious injury.

"She's developed an infection in her lungs. They knew it was a possibility, but we'd honestly hoped she was past the risk at this point."

Warrick didn't try to stop the curse that crossed his lips. "What are they doing about it?"

"Steroids, antibiotics. Monitoring it." Jarrod rubbed at the back of his neck and Warrick knew the stress had to be getting to him.

"Anything on Tyvek?"

Jarrod shook his head. "That's why I'm here. We've still got nothing. The only way that makes sense is if someone is helping him. Or, a lot of someones, maybe."

"Yeah. I'd like to say I'm surprised, but I'm not. He's got a lot of friends, a lot of favors to call in. People might come out in public and say what he did was horrible, but behind closed doors..."

Jarrod looked as sickened by the idea as Warrick felt. "Yeah. If you had to guess who he might have reached out to for help, who can get him out of the country or hide him here, who would your best guess be?"

"I'm afraid that list is going to be longer than you and I would like. Tyvek has an endless number of friends or even just business partners who owe him a lot. And most of them have the deep pockets and resources to help them disappear."

Tyvek's own assets had been frozen as soon as they figured out he was behind the drug testing, so it would be hard for him to have the assets to hide himself easily. He could absolutely be getting help from somebody else, though. Or, it was possible he had assets the government hadn't located. His plot had been planned. It was highly likely he'd set aside resources for getting out when the time came.

"I was afraid of that." Jarrod rubbed the back of his neck. "He's a ghost. He walked out of the fire and vanished into thin air."

"Are you absolutely sure he did walk out of that fire?"

Warrick asked the question that had been needling at the back of his mind.

"Without a doubt. He started several isolated fires in your lab. In each case, the damage to the rooms was contained by the fire department fairly quickly." Jarrod wasn't telling him anything he didn't already know. The property was, after all, his. Well, not his. It belonged to Simms Pharmaceutical. But, he walked through the buildings afterward with his insurance adjusters, once the scene had been cleared. "The fire department found no evidence of a body. In some cases, if a fire burns hot and fast enough, evidence would be hard to detect. Even then, there are ways for us to find human remains. Here, the fire didn't burn hot or fast enough. But even so, once we realized he was missing, I had a human remains detection dog taken through the building. Nothing."

"I guess I just don't want to believe somebody could hide him after what he did."

"You and me both." Jarrod stood. "What do you know about Edward Ball?"

"You think he was involved?" Warrick hated to think that, but he'd discovered recently, not much could surprise him anymore. Meredith and Edward Ball were an unlikely couple, but they seemed to be very much in love. Meredith had dated his Uncle Jonathan a very long time ago, but they'd split up and she'd married Edward shortly after. They'd started Branson Medical together.

"We questioned him before we discovered Tyvek was behind the testing. He seemed innocent, but I've been back to talk to him since Tyvek disappeared and something strikes me as off."

Warrick blew out a breath and thought back on all he

knew about Edward Ball. "I don't know. I know he and Jonathan aren't entirely fond of each other, given Meredith Ball's past with Jonathan. They aren't open enemies or anything, though. Other than that, our contact has all been at business events and things. Up until now, our companies haven't sold the same things. They're in medical devices. We're in pharmaceuticals. We'll be expanding that shortly, but that's a new development."

"During our investigation, we heard rumors that Branson medical was thinking of entering the pharmaceuticals business." Jarrod left the statement out there.

"I'd heard that a while back, but nothing's come of it. I think that was Meredith pushing for it. She wants to grow the business. As far as I know, Edward doesn't have as much interest in it. Although, to be honest, from what I know, he'd do just about anything for her."

Jarrod's brows went up and Warrick realized what he'd said. He shook his head. "I'm sure there are limits to what he'd do. I didn't mean he'd be involved in this."

"Anyone else Tyvek is close to?"

Warrick sighed. "There are some families we all spent a lot of time with at the Cape growing up. The Cabreras and the Danvers still have houses out there. Tyvek spent a lot of time with Mike Caverly and his wife Dot. They live in Hamden and their daughter was friends with Vicki growing up." He thought for a minute more. "Hell, my mom was as close to him as anyone." Warrick frowned. He'd like to be able to say his mom would never help Tyvek out, but his family was so damned screwed up. He wouldn't put it past her.

"Do you really think your mother would help him?" Jarrod asked.

Warrick just looked at him and gave a shrug of his shoulders. "I'd like to think no one would."

Jarrod nodded. "All right. If you think of anyone else we should look into, let me know?"

Warrick nodded. "You got it." He wanted Tyvek off the street. Carrie and he had been good friends since they were young. He hated to think Tyvek had almost killed her, and the thought that he might go after her again had been hanging over him. He was sure it must be keeping Jarrod up at nights.

Jarrod stood to leave, but turned back as he reached the door. "Hey, I saw Jack Sutton and he told me about the prosthetics project. You should talk to Jax Cutter about that. See if he has ideas. And maybe talk to Carrie. She said a lot of space at the shelter now isn't being used. Maybe she can help set you up with a way to distribute these. Maybe a monthly clinic?"

Warrick nodded, but his gut tightened. Could he really go to the very place where all this had started and ask them for help?

* * *

"It's okay," Tyvek said to himself, not concerned if anyone overheard him, as he watched her walk away.

It was funny. People used to look at him. They saw him the minute they walked into the room. People said he commanded attention. Respect. At one time, it had been important to him.

Nowadays, people looked right through him. He'd worked hard to make it that way. He'd had to choose whether to run or stay and take down Warrick. He'd chosen to stay, but it hadn't been easy to hide. It had meant twisting more arms, more leverage. But it was worth it if it meant his Vicki was coming back to him.

It was okay now. He'd found her. She was back and she was okay. She was hiding, just like him, but she'd hadn't run from him this time. She was older now, the grown-up Vicki, and not exactly the same, but she'd come home to him.

CHAPTER 5

THE SOLUTION HAD BEEN SIMPLE. Sara had started coming in later and working later. Of course, she still had to see Warrick during the workday, but she saw less of him. He was an early bird. Honestly, that was her preferred work time also. But she found she focused better if she just avoided him. So she came in at eleven and worked until eight o'clock. She'd always had a lot of autonomy shifting between different worksites for Jack Sutton. It was one of the things she liked about the job.

When she got in at eleven, most of the staff left for lunch soon after and she had a good hour or two to focus on her own. If she had any questions for Warrick, she met with him briefly after lunch, then went back down to her office on the lower level. It meant they saw each other once a day at most.

It also gave her a solid two hours of peace and quiet in the evening when nobody else was around. Sara liked quiet. She'd always been that way, always able to work better on her own without people around to pester her. In fact, in the military, it had been a huge struggle to get used to working as a team, and she still preferred to work on her own if given the choice.

She stretched her neck from side to side trying to work the kinks out, and glanced at the clock. She hadn't realized she'd worked quite that late. She was usually pretty good about leaving by eight or eight-thirty at the latest. Today though, she made a lot of progress on one of the reports Warrick had asked her to put together. She'd begun to realize that he knew what he was doing. He was analyzing her product left to right, inside and out, in ways she hadn't even thought about. And he'd actually managed to shave time and money off of production. When she'd seen he'd done it without diminishing the quality, she'd been impressed.

She turned back to her computer. If she stayed another half an hour she could get this finished up, drop it upstairs for Warrick and still be home by midnight. And then she probably wouldn't need to see him tomorrow.

Yes, avoiding him was stupid, but Samantha had put ideas into her head that she was doing everything she could not to think about. It wasn't working, but she was trying. Avoidance seemed like the best policy right now.

Twenty minutes later, Sara stepped out of the elevator and walked down the hall toward Warrick's office.

"Come on, let's just get you to the couch. I don't think I could get you to my car myself, so you have to sleep it off here for a while."

Sara stopped in the doorway, unsure of what to do. Maybe it wasn't too late to walk away. She knew who the man was. She'd seen his picture plenty of times in the paper over the last few months, but she had yet to meet Jonathan Simms. He was no longer working with the company. After the scandal had hit the papers, and his involvement had come out, he had resigned pretty quickly. Simms Pharmaceutical was a family company, but he had betrayed that family when he'd shown William Tyvek the formula to a drug that ultimately allowed Tyvek to frame Warrick Staunton.

From the looks of things, Staunton and Simms were still talking. Well, not so much talking. Simms was currently struggling to get an extremely inebriated Staunton over to the couch.

Sara took one step backward, thinking to walk away without being seen, then thought better of it when she saw Simms nearly go down under the weight of the younger man. Jonathan Simms was tall, but he was a lot thinner than Warrick. And he was much older. In fact, he looked older than the pictures she'd seen of him in the news only months before.

"I've got him," Sara said as she moved forward and slipped herself under Warrick's other arm.

Warrick turned to her, eyes dazed. "Did you know? When you got in that car, Vicki, did you know about her?"

Simms grunted under the weight of Warrick even though Sara was now taking a great deal of it on herself. "Ignore him. He only drinks hard alcohol once a year, but when he does, he hits it hard. Help me get him over here."

Together they wrestled Warrick over to the couch where he slumped down, but continued to look at her. He didn't say anything more as Simms took off his shoes and slid him over so he laid with his head on one arm of the couch. Simms busied himself lifting Warrick's legs onto the other side, arranging him as best you could arrange a man his size on the couch meant to seat two.

Now anger crossed Warrick's face. "You should have fought harder. You should have tried harder."

"Sleep it off Warrick," Simms said, ushering Sara out of the office with one hand on her shoulder. He shut the door behind them, then turned to apologize. "Sorry about that. I had a feeling he might not get himself home for that this year, what with selling the house and all. He's got the condo to go to of course, but I figured I would check here for him."

"This year?" Sara didn't know why she was asking anything. She should go. She could give the report to him at work in the morning.

"He does this every year. It's the anniversary of his wife's death. Only time he drinks." Simms looked back at the office door and ran a hand through his hair. "I'll stick around a few hours then see if I can wake him up and drive him home. Thank you for your help. I'm Warrick's uncle, Jonathan." He extended his hand and she shook it, still a little stunned at what she'd just witnessed. She honestly wasn't sure what to think of Simms. The employees here talked about him as if he were greatly missed. They made him sound like he was Santa Claus or something. Always happy, always kind and friendly to everyone.

To her, he was partly responsible for a number of people being killed, including veterans. She was friends with Jax Cutter, who had lost his best friend, Leo Kent. Leo had been a Marine at one time, but battles with PTSD and alcohol had led him to the streets. He'd been one of the men killed by William Tyvek.

She couldn't help but feel Jonathan Simms should have foreseen something. Then again, who would've foreseen what William Tyvek had done? Still, going to him with the formula that was proprietary just because his own company had decided they wouldn't work on the drug any longer, had been the catalyst for everything that had happened from there.

"Sara Blackburn." She shook his hand. "Why was he calling me Vicki back there?" She tilted her head toward the door and fought the urge to shiver at the strange feeling she had.

"It's nothing," Simms said. "His wife's name was Vicki." He squinted his eyes at Sara. "I guess you do have her eyes. It's not the exact eye color or anything like that. It's hard to put my finger on it. Her hair was a completely different color and her face was a different shape. But there's something about your eyes that look just like hers."

Sara took a step back. It was odd being told you looked like a dead woman. Or rather didn't exactly look like a dead woman, but sort of looked like her. The whole incident was odd and she wanted nothing more than to get out of there.

"Okay, well I'm just going to get going."

He didn't argue, nor did he say anything as she walked toward the elevators. She looked back and saw him settle himself on one of the lobby couches. She'd be lying to herself if she said she wouldn't spend the ride home wondering what Warrick's questions had meant.

CHAPTER 6

WARRICK KNOCKED on the door frame of Sara's open office. "Got a minute?"

She swiveled in her chair to face him. "Sure, what's up?"

He had to hand it to her, she was doing a damned good job of acting like nothing happened the night before. He was grateful for her performance. The physical effects of his night were killing him, but worse, he was embarrassed anyone besides Jonathan had seen him that way.

He glanced over his shoulder and stepped in. "I just wanted to say I'm..." He paused, not really sure what to say here. He never had to apologize to someone who worked for him for making a fool of himself, for putting them in the uncomfortable situation of seeing him not only wasted, but falling down.

"I just wanted to say I'm sorry for last night. It was completely unprofessional and it won't happen again." God, he sounded like an ass.

She nodded and turned back to her computer, apparently either not bothered in the least by his behavior or not caring if he apologized.

He stood there for a minute trying to figure out how to tell her the rest of it. No, tell was wrong. He wouldn't tell her anything. He hadn't shared anything with anyone about his wife or what had happened the night his wife had died. But for some reason he needed her to know that what she was thinking wasn't right. Because he knew exactly what it would sound like.

"I just want you to know I wasn't talking about a mistress."

Now she spun with her mouth open. "I'm sorry, what?"

He rubbed his forehead. "Shit. Look, I'm screwing this all up. I just wanted you to know I wasn't cheating on my wife." He remembered what he'd said last night in his drunken stupor and it had hit him earlier that it would sound very much like he'd been having an affair. Vicki and he had had their issues—Lord knew they had their issues— but he never in a million years would've cheated on his wife. He didn't know why, but he wanted Sara to know that. "I loved my wife. I never cheated on her. I just want you to know that. It's important to me that people know that."

"Okay." She nodded again and turned away from him, but turned back almost as quickly. "So who were you talking about? Who is the her?" She stilled for a moment as she seemed to realize what she'd just asked, and shook her head. "No, sorry, never mind. Don't answer that. It's not my business and I don't need to know."

Which was good, since he could never say the words. He shoved his hands in his pockets and took her at her word, changing the subject without answering her question. "I got your report on the manufacturing set-up. We'll need a facility that lets us come fit the prostheses and helps us match up with people who need them. I was thinking we might talk to Carrie about using some of the extra space she has at the shelter."

"She has extra space at the shelter?"

Warrick nodded and walked into the office, taking one of the chairs she had in front of her desk and sinking down into it. His body felt wrecked from the treatment he'd given it last night, and he realized he should have brought his water bottle down with him. He needed to hydrate if he was going to get through the day. "With Connecticut's new initiatives to end chronic homelessness, the shelter actually has open space. She was planning to turn a lot of it into additional clinic space. Of course, they have a lot of bad press to overcome right now, so that might not be an option any more. Honestly, they're probably suffering more in this whole thing than we are. They lost a lot of funding. I was able to make some of it up, but of course the Tyvek contributions are gone, and many other small contributors have walked away after the scandal."

"Yeah, well, having your doctors test on their homeless constituents will do that to you."

Warrick looked up sharply. "Carrie had no idea. I swear to you, she's a good person."

"I believe you. I know she didn't know what was going on. You have to be honest though, that in and of itself is a little troubling. The fact she and the director had no idea this was happening doesn't exactly speak well about their ability to do their jobs."

Sara wondered if she should just quit her job right now. She seemed to have an inability to keep her mouth shut when she should keep her opinions to herself. She watched Warrick's face and saw the flicker of anger in his eyes, but also saw him get it under control. With the exception of last night, control seemed to be what he excelled at. She wondered if he ever let any of that emotion out.

Not that she cared.

Warrick nodded slowly. "I see your point, but they are good at what they do. Even the other doctors didn't seem to know what was happening." He sighed. "I don't know if it would help matters or hurt things if we continue to get involved with the clinic. I mean, it could help if we were there once a month fitting veterans with free prostheses. Or, people could see it as a bad thing that the clinic would still be involved with us after everything that happened."

"If it's a chance the shelter is willing to take, I guess you should take advantage of that. And it's not like there's any danger to the veterans here. We're helping them by giving them a free prosthesis. They could spin it as them reaffirming their commitment to help veterans and those in need." Sara fidgeted with the pencil on her desk with her right hand. He made her nervous, and she didn't like to think about why that was.

Sara hadn't thought about sex since her fiancé had walked out of her hospital room a month after she'd come home from her overseas tour. At least not sex where someone else was involved in the equation. She blamed Samantha for the thoughts that ran through her head every time she saw Warrick. Samantha had been the one to put the ideas there. Ideas about what he would look like under that suit. What he would be like if he let loose. What being in bed with him would be like.

Hot. Hot as hell is what it would be like. It didn't take a genius to see that. A man couldn't look like he did, move the way he did, and have the confidence he did without taking command in bed. Sara squirmed in her chair at the thought.

"You seem like you don't want to be here," he said, tilting his head and studying her with those eyes that overwhelmed her.

Sara swallowed and caught herself. For a minute, she'd thought he could see right through her. That he could see she wanted to be in bed, not in the office. She had to push down the laughter as she realized he meant at Simms, working on the project with him. Well, that much was true. She still had mixed feelings on that one.

"The jury's out," she said, not offering more.

She hoped that would be it, but he sat there, watching her. She could see the challenge in his eyes. He wasn't saying it, but he was calling her a chicken for not telling him more. Those damned eyes of his said everything.

She huffed. "I don't like feeling like a poster child for gimps just so you and the shelter can save your asses."

He watched her for a minute, then nodded. "Cool, then we'll cast you as the smart-as-hell hottie who built her own prostheses and is sharing that technology with the world for free."

He stood and walked out, leaving her staring after him with her chin on the floor.

Hottie?

CHAPTER 7

WARRICK LOOKED down at the bag of potting soil and tried to judge if he'd put enough in the giant planter he'd set in the corner of the room. He looked up at the sun shining through the French doors and hoped it would be enough. The woman at the gardening center had told him he might have enough sun for the rose bush on the south-facing patio. She'd also assured him this was the right kind of soil and the ceramic planter was large enough to let the rose flourish for the next couple of years until he had a yard to plant it in again. He hoped so. The pot was as big around as a tractor tire and as tall as his hip.

He tugged at the knot on the burlap wrapped around the root ball, loosening it before lifting it into the pot.

"Warrick! You here?" His Uncle Jonathan walked through the living room.

"Yeah. Out here!" Warrick wiped at his brow with the back of one hand, then looked at the dirt on his pants and shirt. He probably should have changed out of his work clothes for this. He'd taken off his coat and tie, but his dress shirt and pants didn't need this kind of abuse. Maybe he should get rid of his suits. He shouldn't really need to dress like a damned banker. He owned the company. He could put a business casual dress code in at work and be done with it. He was sure none of his employees would object.

"What are you doing?" From the tone, his uncle sounded like he'd caught him milking a cow in his condo instead of planting a rose.

"Transplanted it from the house." He didn't turn around as he answered, but instead busied himself packing the soil around the roots and pressing it into place. "Shit."

"What?" His uncle came and peered with Warrick at the soil in the planter.

"I was supposed to add water before I topped off the soil."

"Does it matter?"

Warrick didn't know. "The woman at the gardening place told me to do it that way."

"You could scoop out the dirt, then water it and put it back." The two stood staring at the plant, as though the answer might appear in the dirt.

"She said keep the disruption to a minimum. Apparently, roses stress easily." Warrick lifted the bucket he'd filled with water and poured it around the base of the bush.

"Roses stress?" Jonathan looked perplexed.

"Apparently," Warrick repeated. He added more water to the planter, then set down the bucket and went to the kitchen, trailed by Jonathan. Things hadn't been the same between them since Warrick discovered Jonathan shared confidential information from Simms Pharmaceutical with William Tyvek. It had felt like a punch to the gut to find out Jonathan had supplied the information Tyvek had used to kill people and frame Warrick, even though he'd done it unwittingly.

But, aside from his mother and some distant cousins, Jonathan was Warrick's only family. He wouldn't be having a family of his own, he thought, as his eyes cut back to the rose bush on the patio. Their family line would be coming to an end with him. As dramatic as that seemed, for a family like his, it was a big deal. Another way he'd let his father down.

He'd never forget the fight he had with his dad only days before his dad had died. It didn't matter that cancer was kicking his ass. His dad had still wanted to tell Warrick he was letting him down. Not having a son to carry on the Staunton name or even a daughter to carry the Simms and Staunton blood had topped the list.

"Even your prick can't get it right," his dad had said with a laugh, right in front of one of his nurses. His dad had always been crude and blasé where "the staff" was concerned. To him, anyone who worked for them was *the staff*, even if she was a highly skilled nurse making sure he was as comfortable as possible in his last days. As far as his father was concerned, she was being paid to ignore anything she heard. This particular nurse had rolled her eyes behind his father's back in what Warrick guessed was an attempt to make him feel better.

He'd appreciated it, even though he hadn't cared much that his father thought his "prick" wasn't good enough. What he'd cared about was that, in his father's final hours, they still couldn't find a way to connect. He'd left the room, and his father had slipped into a coma shortly after.

He hadn't woken up.

Warrick pulled himself from his thoughts and rinsed his hands, watching the dirt run down the kitchen drain. "Beer?" He asked his uncle, then grabbed two from the fridge when he received an answering nod.

"You're going to leave, aren't you?"

His uncle's question made him pause, beer halfway to his mouth. "What do you mean?"

Jonathan smiled, but there was pain and sadness behind it. "I can see you've got one foot out the door. You're planning to pull the company out of the tailspin and then leave, aren't you?"

Warrick set down his beer and nodded. "Yeah, probably." He and his uncle had always been close. In fact, sometimes it amazed Warrick that his mom and his uncle had been raised by the same people. His mom hadn't had time for him. She and his dad liked to travel. They'd been happy to have other people raise him.

But Uncle Jonathan had always been there for Warrick. Sure, he was a bit of a spacey guy at times, burying himself in the lab when something caught his focus. But, for the most part, he'd been there for Jonathan when his parents hadn't.

His uncle looked sad now, and Warrick hoped he wasn't going to apologize again. He didn't know if he could take that. He knew Jonathan was sorry. And he forgave him. The only problem was, the wound had cut deep. It would take time to scar over.

"Where will you go?"

Warrick shrugged. "I don't know. I'm not even sure I'll go anywhere. I might just stay here and do something new."

Now Jonathan's eyes lit. "Is something calling to you?"

Warrick laughed. Jonathan had always talked about the way science called to him. He'd wanted that for Warrick, but Warrick hadn't felt that same draw to anything. He was meant to lead the family company. That was what his role was. His dad had never had an interest in running it. He'd wanted to spend the money it supplied, but that was it.

Warrick had plunged neck deep into running the business when his turn had come.

"Sorry, Uncle Jonathan. Nothing is calling to me."

"So what will you do?"

"I have no idea. I just know I shouldn't be doing this anymore."

Before his uncle could say anything more, the doorbell rang. Warrick wasn't expecting anyone. In fact, not a lot of people knew where his new place was. Not that he had people visit him at his house even when he lived at the old address.

His uncle followed him out toward the door. "Oh, that'll be Jack, Andrew, and Chad."

"Excuse me?" Warrick turned to look at his uncle.

"Open it, open it." Jonathan waved his hands toward the door. "They're here to pick you up."

"Pick me up for what?" Warrick asked as he swung open the door.

"Basketball." Andrew Weston walked through the door, flanked by Jack Sutton and Chad Thompson. Jack was the one that Warrick knew best, having worked with him a few times as Sutton Capital took on its new role with Simms Pharmaceutical. He'd met Andrew Weston, Sutton Capital's chief financial officer and Chad Thompson, Sutton's head of security and Jack's cousin, during the negotiations. He liked all three of the men, but he hadn't expected them to show up on his doorstep.

"And we don't have much time," Jack said. "We need to be on the court by seven."

Andrew looked at Warrick's clothes. "It's an interesting look," he said, no doubt in reference to the dirt that still clung to the front of Warrick's suit. "I'm afraid it's not going to work for basketball."

"Uh." Warrick looked at the three men, then back to Jonathan. "What?"

"He didn't tell you we were coming, did he?" Chad asked with a grin. "You were supposed to tell him we were coming." He turned toward Jonathan Simms.

"I hadn't gotten to it yet." Jonathan shrugged. "Anyone want a beer while Warrick changes?" Jonathan had a way of making friends with everyone.

"You realize I haven't played basketball since..." He cut off. He couldn't remember the last time he played basketball. Probably in prep school, maybe college.

"That's okay." Andrew clapped him on the back. "You're playing for the other team. They tried to cancel because they're a man short, but your uncle volunteered you."

"When did this all happen?" Warrick knew the three men had come by Simms that afternoon to tour some of the facility, but he hadn't realized his Uncle Jonathan had been in the office at the time.

"This afternoon." Jonathan looked at his watch. "You better get moving. Who knows, maybe your future is in the NBA."

Warrick rolled his eyes, but he left the room to change. What was the worst that could happen?

CHAPTER 8

WARRICK WAS ABOUT AS SKILLED with crutches as he was on the basketball court. Not at all. He winced at the memory. He probably shouldn't have tried a jump shot with Chad guarding him. It was about as hopeless as trying a jump shot against Shaquille O'Neal. Chad was a seriously big man.

As for the crutches, it wasn't that he couldn't get around on them. It was that he didn't want to. The slowness of them did nothing but irritate him. He tossed one of them toward the couch in his office and proceeded to hobble, leaning on the remaining crutch. The air cast on his ankle was awkward, but he was able to walk on it.

"I'm pretty sure that's not what they meant when they said 'use crutches.'"

He knew Sara's voice immediately by the way his body involuntarily reacted to it. She had one of those voices straight out of an old movie, throaty and sexy as shit. He cursed under his breath, reminding his body he didn't appreciate the reaction to her.

Not to mention the kick to his ego at her seeing him like

this. Why the hell did it bother him so much to have her see him as weak in any way? He shouldn't care.

He turned as he got to his chair and sank into it, letting the other crutch drop to the floor beside him. Glaring at it made him feel better. It also let him ignore her a little longer while he willed his dick back into line.

"Here." She held out an ice pack wrapped in a towel. "Charlotte told me to tell you, it's time to ice and elevate."

He grunted and took the ice pack, but tossed it on the desk instead of lifting his leg to ice it.

Sara tilted her head at him and he saw an uncharacteristic playfulness cross her face. At least, it wasn't an expression she had around him very often. Maybe she was more at ease with her friends.

"I should have known you'd be a bad patient," she said. She sat in the chair opposite him and settled in.

"Why is that?" He focused on pulling up the files he'd need for their meeting, keeping his eyes on the computer screen instead of her. He didn't want to admit, even to himself, that he liked it when she teased him. He liked the feeling that maybe she liked him. What was he? A teenager?

The thought brought back a memory of him waiting behind the bleachers for Vicki to sneak out of study hall and meet him. The memory served as cold water, shaking him out of the stupor Sara had put him in.

"You just strike me as someone who'd never want to slow down long enough to heal. I was the same way after my injury. The physical therapists actually had to try to slow me down, instead of pumping me up to try one more rep of an exercise."

He hadn't ever heard her talk about her injury or her

recovery. He turned her way. "Did it work? Did they get you to slow down?"

"Nope." Her smile was wicked as she laughed, but she gestured to the ice pack. "You should still ice it."

With an exaggerated glare that she rewarded with a laugh, he grabbed the ice pack, lifted his leg to the extra chair Charlotte had placed by his desk, and followed her direction. "You have a twisted sense of humor."

He wondered what it had felt like for Sara to go through months of recovery and learning to use her prosthesis. He was frustrated from this little sprain. Embarrassed and worrying about what she might think of him. What was it like for her when she came home and had to face the loss of her hand? He couldn't imagine the frustration she must have dealt with learning how to use a prosthesis to do things most people took for granted.

He almost asked, but they weren't close enough for that question.

"What happened, anyway?" She asked. "There are all kinds of rumors going around. Everything from skydiving accident to a mishap with a mechanical bull." Her eyes said she was enjoying this a little too much.

"Seriously?" Why on earth would anyone be coming up with that kind of shit, much less talking about his injury in the first place?

"Yup. Renee over in accounting is guessing it happened during kinky BDSM role playing that went awry, but she's a little obsessed with Fifty Shades, if you ask me."

Warrick stared blankly at Sara. He was sure his brain was attempting automatic shutdown so he didn't have to acknowledge the fact his employees were imagining him in a BDSM dungeon. It wasn't working.

"I—" He stopped and just stared at her. "What?"

This made Sara laugh harder.

He should make sure she knew it hadn't been some crazy BDSM experiment gone wrong. Shouldn't he? "Basketball," he said abruptly.

And she laughed harder.

CHAPTER 9

SARA CROSSED THE PARK, balancing a tray of small coffees in her hand. She'd had to get out of the building, to get away and clear her head. One minute, she'd been laughing with Warrick, and the next...well, she didn't know what happened. The energy in the room shifted somehow. It had become charged, and the charge had come directly from the energy zipping back and forth between them. It had thrown her off.

He'd noticed it too. She'd seen the minute he became aware of the shift, and he hadn't seemed any happier about it than she'd been.

She steadied the tray of drinks with the stump of her left arm as she scanned the park. She was giving her arm a break from the prosthesis while she was out. One thing she'd noticed, no one in the homeless population seemed to bat an eye at her stump. Some of her friends didn't either, and it was what had drawn her to them. Samantha, for example, hadn't been the least bit phased by seeing the portion of Sara's forearm that was thinner than it should have been, where the muscle had been torn right from the bone. She didn't seem to mind the angry scarring or any of that. Instead, Samantha had been immediately fascinated with helping Sara design her prostheses. They'd calculated figures together and tried various attachments, without any of the unease she typically found when engaging with new people. It was why the two were close friends now.

The first time she'd shown the slightest bit of hesitation at removing her prosthesis, Samantha had taken care of the issue. In true Samantha style, her friend lifted her shirt clear up to her neck, flashing her breasts at Sara. It brought the laughter Samantha was likely hoping for. It also exposed the crescent-shaped scars that topped each breast, a result of Samantha's horrific run-in with armed mercenaries sent to kidnap her.

"There." Samantha had pulled her shirt back into place. "We're good now. Take it off."

Sara shook off the memory as she spotted a small group of people in the park and recognized two of the three faces. Darla was one of them. She thought one of the men might be named Matt, or maybe Dave. She didn't know the other one at all. She headed that way and offered the coffee silently to the group. All three took a cup, nodding their thanks.

"You goin' go broke, you keep this up," Darla offered, but her smile and the way she wrapped her hands around the cup told Sara a different story. Darla was no longer homeless thanks to Connecticut's zero homelessness initiative. She had recently moved into a room at a local place, but she came out and spent most days with her friends. She'd told Sara she couldn't stand to look at four walls when she wasn't asleep.

"I'll tell my boss I need a raise," she said, smiling back, before walking toward the other end of the park. One man sat alone on a bench. She didn't know his name yet, and he seemed to keep clear, even of the others. She had a feeling interacting with people was hard for him. He seemed to be living inside his own head most of the time.

Sara approached slowly, and waited until the older man looked at her. He seemed to look through her for a minute, then his face brightened with recognition, and she moved forward, her hand outstretched to offer the last of the cups of coffee.

"You came back," he said, a somewhat reverent disbelief in his voice. He didn't move to take the coffee, so Sara pulled it from the wedged spot on the tray and set it next to him on the bench, then sat down on the other side of it.

"I said I would." She looked at him and ignored the smell emanating from him. A heavy beard covered most of his face. It was yellowed as if the grime and soil had soaked in to discolor it permanently, and she felt a tug at her heart. Her grandfather had had trouble caring for himself when he'd gotten older, having a hard time bathing or even remembering to bathe. Her grandfather had the benefit of family to help him though. She wondered if this man had anyone.

She'd also seen him favor the right side of his body, and she wondered if he had been in an accident. She'd never ask about it. It wasn't any of her business. She never questioned the people she brought meals or coffee to out in the park.

She hadn't talked with this man much, but he didn't strike her as a veteran. Still, he'd seen things in life, she would guess. Been hurt, and not just physically. There was a bone deep pain she recognized in him.

"Drink the coffee," she said. "It'll warm you up." It wasn't the kind of brittle cold weather they'd see during the winter yet, but they were certainly having a cold snap, and sitting on the cold bench hour after hour had to get to a body after a bit.

He nodded, but didn't pick up the cup. He simply smiled at her, and she wondered if he'd had much company since showing up in town. Darla had told her he was new in New Haven. He'd shown up a month ago, but hadn't seemed to want to engage with many of them. Darla had passed this information on without judgement, but now Sara wondered about it. He certainly hadn't seemed hesitant to talk to Sara.

"Will you come back again?" He asked, and Sara nodded, then turned to look at the park. She wondered what he watched as he sat on the bench. She'd seen him on this bench before.

Sara glanced toward the sky, but her eyes caught on the figure in the large window at the top floor of Simms Pharmaceutical. *Warrick*. He stood and looked out over the park, seeming as though he might be looking straight at her. He shoved his hands in his pockets and turned away.

"You'll come back?" The man asked again.

Sara nodded, wanting to offer some reassurance. "I'm Sara. What's your name?"

"Buddy. You can call me Buddy."

"I have to go now, Buddy, but I'll come back and see you again." She stood and pushed the coffee closer to him on the bench. He smiled, seeming to snap out of whatever memories had gripped him moments before, and picked up the cup this time. He sipped and Sara smiled at him and waved, before turning back toward the building.

* * *

Tyvek watched as she walked away. It was her. She was

back. She was different this time, but her eyes were the same. He would always know her eyes. It wasn't the color of the brown eyes they both shared. In fact Vicki's had been a little lighter. It was the kindness in the eyes. His Vicki had always had that kindness in her. She was too kind. He was beginning to see that.

He looked at the Simms Pharmaceutical building and scowled. He had hoped she'd be strong enough this time. That she would walk away from the temptation Warrick held, but she'd never been strong where Warrick Staunton was concerned. Even as a teenager, she'd been drawn to Warrick like he was some kind of drug.

Not this time. Tyvek hadn't been firm enough with her before. This time, he'd make sure she wasn't drawn in again.

CHAPTER 10

"YOU CONNECT with them in a way most people don't."

Sara turned in her seat to face Warrick as he drove them out to the site where her prostheses would be manufactured. His statement had come out of nowhere and she truly had no idea what he was talking about. "Back it up and give me the whole conversation this time."

He let out a huff of laughter and shook his head. "Sorry. Yesterday. I saw you talking to the homeless man in the park. You go there a lot to talk to them. You seem to connect with them. I was just wondering why."

Sara shrugged and turned back to the road. "They're just people."

"True." He didn't offer any more.

She was more surprised than she'd care to admit when the next words came out of her mouth. "Transients are safe. They don't expect me to stick around and I don't expect them to stick around."

The weight of her admission hung in the air around them as Warrick pulled into the drive of the old Simms compound. They were now calling it Simms II even though it was Simms I if you thought about it. It was the original Simms Pharmaceutical building.

Part of her got the creeps any time they came to the site, knowing a woman had been left to burn here a month before. She'd been saved, but the event was troubling nonetheless. Sara had met Carrie Hastings and the man who'd saved her, Jarrod Harmon. He was a detective who was friends with Jack Sutton and Jack's cousin Chad. Carrie had seemed nice, although they hadn't talked much. Sara and Samantha had been having coffee one day when the couple had come in and stopped by to say hello to Samantha. When Samantha introduced them, Sara realized who they were.

Warrick parked in front of the lab that was being converted into the facility to produce her prostheses and they stepped out. He was still wearing an air cast on his ankle, but he'd abandoned the crutches.

The old administration building was being refurbished and would be leased out to other companies. The building William Tyvek had set on fire was being torn down. Warrick planned to wait on building anything on the site until he had a lessee for it so the new structure could be custom designed for whoever leased it.

The foreman on the project met them at the temporary chain metal fence surrounding the structure and handed them each a hard hat to put on. The gesture sent a memory through Sara and she remembered putting her protective helmet on her head hundreds of times when she was deployed. It didn't take much for that memory to warp into the sight of her helmet lying on the ground beside her when she'd been thrown from the armored vehicle she'd been in the day she lost her hand. A roadside bomb. The smoke and noise. Everything had sounded muffled, the way things sound when you're in the bathtub and you submerge your ears under the water.

She stood still, her hands on the hard hat as she remembered the feeling of looking around her. Seeing the others in her unit. Feeling relief that Johnson and Danners were all right. Then turning when they shouted and ran toward her. Looking to her left to see who they were running for. The realization they were running for her. Because her arm...no, not her arm. Blood. A bloody stump where her hand should have been. She'd moved it then, pulling it away from where the truck lay. The pain had roared through her as she put two and two together and her brain kicked into gear. Her stomach had twisted as bile raced up her throat and she lost the contents of her stomach. The hand that should have been there was now under the truck. She could see it. See the ligaments, torn muscle and bits of cellulose.

"Sara!" Warrick shook her gently, as he called to her and she snapped back.

It wasn't Johnson and Danners calling to her. They had called her Blackburn that day, just as they always had. They were protective of her, as the only woman in their unit. They'd called to her and told her to hang tight while they got her out of there. And they had. They'd gotten her right out to safety and treatment, and she'd gone home.

"Sara," Warrick said, quietly now as the foreman moved away, giving them space at Warrick's hard glance. "Are you okay?"

Sara nodded. She didn't have flashbacks anymore. Not in a long time, but she knew they'd probably come once in a blue moon forever. It was something she accepted and lived with. Nothing that had happened to her overseas would ever go away entirely. She forced a smile. "I'm good. We can go in now."

Warrick studied her and she scowled at him. "Go. Now." She pointed to the building. She hated attention on her. And attention from this man made her doubly nervous. She didn't like for anyone to ever see her vulnerable or weak, but the idea of Warrick seeing her that way was even worse.

He seemed so perfect, she mused. Never mind, *seemed*. The man was perfect.

And she was not. Not even close. She tucked her left arm against her side, almost hiding it behind her back, but not quite going that far, and walked toward the building. They were here to check the progress on the room that would house the techs charged with assembling the prostheses and testing each of the hands as they came off the line.

"Everything's on schedule?" Warrick asked the foreman, who fell in line alongside them again as they entered the building. Sara couldn't believe how fast they'd been able to repurpose the rooms and put together clean rooms for the manufacturing and assembly. Half of the building was finished already and the components of her hands were being fabricated on 3D printers that were twice as large and much faster than the one she'd been working on during the design phase.

"Just barely," the foreman said. "It's a hell of a schedule."

Warrick didn't apologize for the schedule. Sara had a feeling he didn't apologize for anything in his life and she realized somewhere along the way, her view of him had begun to change. She'd thought he was this trust fund guy who's had everything given to him, but the truth was, he seemed to be busting his ass to make sure his employees had a job at the end of the month. She had to respect that.

She reminded herself he was still responsible for testing a drug that had ended up killing five of their test subjects. She needed to keep her distance here.

Why? A little voice inside her head asked.

She didn't need to list the reasons for the voice, but she did anyway. Because she was attracted to the man. And that was not okay. Not on any planet or in any scenario was it okay for her to fall for a man again. Especially this man.

It may have been years since her fiancé walked away from her, but the look on his face when he'd looked at the stump where her hand used to be would stick with her forever. They hadn't even gotten to the point where she might ever touch him with it, or where it might ever brush against him while they shared a bed. She could only imagine his response then. It wasn't hard to imagine. He would have been disgusted.

Sara pushed thoughts of Mitchell away and wandered down the hall to look through the viewing windows into the production room. Three technicians checked the machines and busied themselves as the 3D printers whirred. Trays held various pieces ready to be assembled, and Sara smiled at the colors they'd chosen to print. There was her purple alongside a bright pink, bright blue, deep gray, rich brown, and a white that was almost clear, letting the user see the inner workings of the hand.

She moved further down and saw a printer working on child-sized prostheses. That had been Warrick's idea. They would distribute them to children needing prostheses and charge on a sliding scale according to the family's ability to pay. The colors for the child sizes were the bright pink and purple, as well as a red and blue one that reminded Sara of Spiderman and a yellow that looked like melted crayon.

She felt Warrick when he came up behind her. She had noticed that started happening. At least he couldn't sneak up on her anymore, but honestly being able to feel him behind her wasn't a great feeling either. It meant she'd become too aware of him. Her body reacted involuntarily to him. She turned and found him watching her. He glanced over her shoulder through the room and seemed to be assessing the progress for a minute, but she could see he wasn't only in businessman mode right now like he usually was. She had noticed that about him lately. There seemed to be something different about him.

Whatever he had been looking for in the room, he apparently found it, because he refocused on her. Once again, Sara felt the unwanted response her body seemed to have to him. It was that small tangle of butterflies that started in her belly, the little bit of excitement that comes on a first date. The buzz of the first kiss.

She stepped back. This was not a date. There would be no first kiss. This would not happen.

"Everything okay?" Warrick's question was casual, but his voice was just one note lower on the register than it should have been.

Sara nodded and stepped to the side, turning to face the window, so they were standing side-by-side rather than with her trapped between him and the wall. Not that she wouldn't mind being trapped between him and the wall. *Oh Lord.*

She went from nodding to shaking her head in a matter of seconds, before she realized he wouldn't understand why she was shaking her head. She was shaking her head at herself because of the way her mind kept going to places she didn't want to go with him.

Of course, when she looked over he was eyeing her quizzically.

"You sure about that? Because yes and no at the same time makes me wonder." Now he was laughing at her and she couldn't really blame him.

She cleared her throat. "Yes." She infused the word with as much confidence as she could. Then she turned to him, deciding they needed to focus on business so her mind wouldn't keep going to places it shouldn't be. "I spoke to Marissa in marketing today. She had a great idea for an ad once we're ready to open the prostheses up to the open market."

Warrick turned to her, seeming to take the bait and focus on business. "Yeah? What's that?"

"We put together a video montage showing all of the things this hand can do that other prostheses can't do. Shaking hands, opening a jar, a woman curling her hair with a curling iron. Maybe a child swinging a baseball bat or couple holding hands."

"You couldn't hold hands with the regular prosthesis?"

"No." Sara quickly warmed to her subject. This was something she was comfortable with. She liked talking about the advancements that had been made in the field lately, the new things that her prostheses could do that more traditional prosthetics couldn't. She placed her hands on Warrick's upper arms. "With this prosthesis, I can control the strength and intensity of the grip." She squeezed her natural hand on his upper arm, at the same time making the required movements with her forearm to do the same with her prosthesis where her left hand should have been.

"With this prosthesis, the movement is very similar to

the movement a natural hand makes. With a traditional prosthesis it wouldn't be the same. The fingers don't curl the same way. The grip couldn't be made softly. It was either open or closed, no in between."

It didn't take long for Sara to stop and realized her mistake. They were now standing close together. Too close together. And her hands were on him. On muscles far too strong and enticing. Muscles that shouldn't be hiding under a business suit, yet there they were.

Sara froze and looked at Warrick, realizing she was holding her breath. That breath seemed to vanish altogether when she saw his eyes darken and he somehow seemed to move closer to her. She'd felt this before with him. The moment when it clicked, when the air in the room shifted and they both realized there was something going on that they hadn't been acknowledging.

She dropped her hands, preparing to step back, but he caught her wrists, not even seeming to care that one of them wasn't flesh. He didn't say anything but those eyes never left hers. There was a question in them now as if to ask her what they were doing or why this kept happening. She didn't have any answers for him.

Sara's eyes fell to where one of Warrick's hands had closed around the wrist of her prosthesis and she suddenly felt the need to squirm. She felt like she should apologize for him having to feel rubber and metal and plastic where skin should have been. But when she looked up at him again, the intensity in his face hadn't left. It hadn't been replaced by disgust or discomfort and she found the breath suddenly came back into her lungs. She inhaled deeply. It came easily, that breath.

Then Warrick turned his head slowly toward the window and a thought crossed Sara's mind. They weren't alone. Sure enough, when she turned her head, she found all three of the technicians in the room had stopped the work and were staring back at the two of them.

Warrick leaned close to her ear. Too close. "Later." His voice was a commanding growl that should have been a turn off. Sara wasn't into being bossed around.

Sadly, it wasn't.

CHAPTER 11

WHAT DID "LATER" mean?

Sara leaned back against the couch cushion, drawing her legs up under her. She was still trying to figure out if later meant "we'll talk about this later" or "something's going to happen between us later" because there *had* been something happening.

"Hey, you still listening or have you zoned out again?" Samantha handed Sara a glass of wine, then sat on the other side of the couch.

"Sorry." Sara winced and focused on her friend. She hadn't told Samantha what happened with Warrick and she wasn't sure she wanted to. Maybe she was reading a lot more into it than it was. Samantha wouldn't laugh at her, but she wasn't sure she wanted to embarrass herself if Samantha didn't think what happened was as significant as Sara did.

She distracted herself removing her prosthesis and setting it and the sleeve that went under it next to the couch. She'd been in it all day and her arm needed a break.

"Okay now, tell me what's bothering you." Before Sara

could ask what she meant, a wail came through the baby monitor and Samantha jumped up. "Hold that thought."

Minutes later Samantha buzzed through the room, stopping long enough to pause and hand baby Joey to a startled Sara, then headed for the kitchen.

Sara didn't have time to brace herself for the ache that hit her as Joey settled into her arms, his bottom resting on her left arm, his small head cradled in her right hand. She closed her eyes and focused on the feel of his weight as he snuggled into her, his face brushing against her cheek. The feeling was heaven and hell, all wrapped in one. Because she wouldn't ever have this herself.

Samantha came back with a bottle and held it out to Sara.

"What is that?" Sara didn't move to take the bottle, but Samantha took one of the couch pillows and nestled it next to Sara, then shifted Joey so he leaned onto the pillow.

She pressed the bottle into Sara's hand. "A bottle. Feed him." She moved Sara's hand toward the baby, who eagerly began to drink.

"Wait, don't you breastfeed him?" Joey didn't seem to mind the bottle or the fact that Sara was a bit awkward in juggling the pillow and bottle setup.

"I do." Samantha pointed toward her glass of wine. "But not if I've had a drink in the last hour. I don't usually drink if I expect to need to nurse him, but he woke up early. He's cluster feeding. It's a thing." She shrugged. "I keep some pumped milk in the freezer and he's used to a bottle when the sitter comes."

Sara leveled Samantha with a look. "You've had two sips of wine."

Samantha grinned. "Feeding babies is good for you. It makes you all loosey goosey and happy and shit." She waved her hands around in waves in front of her and Sara couldn't help laughing. But Samantha was right. Feeding a baby was magical.

"All right, now that my baby has you all loosened up and I've plied you with wine, tell me what's got you so distracted."

Sara sighed. It wasn't worth fighting it any more. Samantha was relentless when she wanted her friends to open up. "I think something happened with Warrick. I mean, it did happen. Something happened. I just don't really know what." She was babbling. Not to mention, making no sense whatsoever.

Samantha waved a hand at Joey. "Listen he can't understand what we're saying yet. It's A-okay if you want to get into specifics."

"You're crazy." Sara said this with a smile.

"Point taken. Still, start from the beginning."

Sara recapped the incident at the lab with Warrick, including the employees watching them and his growled warning of "later."

"Ohh, *later* sounds good." Samantha said this with a little shimmy like she was imagining all the things later could entail.

"But maybe he means *later* like we'll talk about what an idiot you are for fantasizing about me like that later. Or we'll talk about how you're fired because you made this uncomfortable between us later. Maybe those are the laters."

Her friend's face softened, the amusement gone. "Tell me what happened with your fiancé, Sara."

Sara looked down at Joey who'd fallen back to sleep in her arms. His tiny mouth was open, the bottle still resting on his tongue. He looked content, happy. He clearly didn't have a care in the world, just the way it should be for him.

Samantha reached over and took him, bringing him to her shoulder where she rubbed and patted his back, bringing out a soft burp. She didn't let up on Sara, though. "Clearly, he left you with rejection issues."

"He left." Sara raised a shoulder. "What more is there to say?"

"How about how he left?"

Sara was quiet for a minute. When Mitchell had left her, she hadn't had any girlfriends around to talk to about it. Her mom had been around but she hadn't told her the details. She'd been in a military rehab facility surrounded by tough soldiers fighting their own battles.

"He was disgusted by my injury," she said, looking at her arm. "He was on leave. He came to see me twice, but I could see the disgust in his eyes. See the way he tried to avoid looking at my arm. I'm pretty sure he didn't even realize he was doing it, but he'd cover it with the sheet when we were talking." She looked at Samantha and laughed, but the sound was bitter. "He'd tuck the sheet around it like he could tuck it away from sight and not have to see it."

"What an idiot!" Samantha's indignation made Sara laugh again, and this time it didn't tastes as sour in her mouth.

When the laughter stopped, she met Samantha's eyes. "It hurt so much." Her admission was only a whisper, but it was out there. For the first time, she'd admitted how much it hurt to see the man she'd thought would be by her side no matter what happened, walk out the door. Walk out of her life.

Samantha took her hand. "I know it did, hon. I know."

"I just don't think I'm ready to risk that again. Not with Warrick. Not with anyone."

"So what are you going to do?"

"I'll keep hanging out with him. I like him. But, I just can't let it go any further, you know?"

Samantha smiled, but there was a sadness to it that told Sara her friend was hoping for her to move past this sooner rather than later. She looked at the baby sleeping on Samantha's shoulder. She wanted the same thing. Unfortunately, she just didn't see herself moving on anytime soon. As much as she put on a good front, she wasn't brave enough to watch a guy walk away from her again.

CHAPTER 12

WARRICK WAS TIRED. So tired. Maybe it was the fight for his company. Maybe it was the fight to resist Sara. But he just wanted a normal, easy night. Working at the office wasn't doing it for him anymore. And resisting Sara was beginning to seem hopeless. He took the stairs down to Sara's floor and was only mildly surprised to find her in her office.

"Pitiful." He leaned against the door jamb and waited for her to look up. Those wide brown eyes met his and kicked his heart into overdrive. Those eyes of hers got him every time.

"You're one to talk," she said. She smiled, but there was a shadow behind her eyes he couldn't decipher. He found himself wanting to.

He told himself he was just being friendly. That this was all part of the plan to practice being a normal guy. To practice hanging out and having friends, but a small part of him was starting to recognize the lie.

"Dinner?"

She hesitated so he pushed. He wanted to be with her. "Come on, dinner never hurt anyone."

"Okay." She shut down her computer and grabbed her keys, sticking them in the small bag she threw over one shoulder.

They walked in silence across to the park. It was quiet, but on the other end a lone hot dog vendor waited to take their orders.

Warrick turned to Sara to let her order.

"Two plain."

He turned back to the vendor. "I'll take two with the works." Warrick looked back at the park where he could see the shadow of a man. It was Sara's homeless friend. "Add another couple of plain dogs and three sodas, please." He pulled out his wallet and handed a few bills to the man. "Keep it," he said, raising a hand when the man began to count out his change.

"Thank you."

Warrick juggled the hot dogs while Sara grabbed the sodas and they headed back into the park. "Here."

They settled on a bench and Sara picked up the extra hot dogs and one of the sodas and walked toward where Warrick had seen her homeless friend. "Buddy?" She called out. "Are you hungry?"

Warrick spotted the man walking away. "Sara." He pointed toward the path leading out of the park on the other side. "There."

"Buddy! Are you hungry?" Sara called to him, but he only sped up.

"Huh." She turned back to Warrick. "Maybe he's not in the mood for company. We can leave it for him here. He might come back after we're gone."

Warrick nodded and she settled next to him on the

bench. The conversation as they ate was easy and light. Too light, Warrick noticed. There was something going on with her. Something she wasn't telling him. But as they talked, her façade seemed to fall away and she relaxed.

"So, tell me why you were at the office on a Saturday. I have an excuse. You got nothing." Warrick cracked open one of the sodas for her.

"There was a time I never would have eaten hot dogs and soda for dinner. I was too much of a health nut." Sara frowned at the food, but took a bite. It was heaven, just as she knew it would be. Somehow the hot dogs you got from a street vendor always tasted better than the ones at home.

"It's good for you." Warrick grinned. "Now, really, why are you working?"

"I don't have an excuse. I was just bored, so I came in to work on the go-go gadget model."

He laughed. "You're calling it that now?"

Now it was her turn to grin. "It's a working name."

"Are you hoping to bring that one to market, too?"

"Maybe." Sara crumpled the foil from her first hot dog and opened her second, then began applying the mustard packets she'd grabbed from the vendor. "It's turning out to be a challenge to get the right pressure and to find a material that allows the telescoping effect without being too heavy."

"Make any progress today?"

She shook her head. "I wanted to run some figures on a material a friend told me about, but I looked into it more when I got here. It looks like it has some of the properties I would need, but over time it would break down too much to be worthwhile. The life of the prosthesis would likely be a year or two at the most."

"Could it work for a child's prosthesis? They're already

going through them at that rate anyway because of growth, right?"

Sara sat up and tilted her head. "Possibly, but there are some kids whose growth rate during any given year wouldn't be fast enough to go through it before the material wears too thin. In those cases, the failures wouldn't only be frustrating, they might be dangerous if the prosthesis gives out unexpectedly."

"True. I hadn't thought of that."

She grinned at him. "It's still fun to try to perfect it for myself. I mean, really, who doesn't want an arm that grows another two or three inches when you need it?"

He laughed. He was doing that a lot more frequently with her.

Warrick leaned in, holding her gaze as he moved closer, giving her a chance to move away. She didn't.

He kissed her. Softly at first, but the small touch of his mouth to hers lit a fire somewhere inside, and he deepened the connection. He reached for her, pulling her closer to him as a small moan escaped her. God, she did things to him.

She raised her hand and ran her fingers through his hair.

The sensation had a primal effect. He didn't care that they were in the middle of the park. He wanted to drag her closer, still. To peel away her clothes and reveal every inch of her. Then to cover her back up. Not with clothes, but with his kisses, his touch, his body.

Why did this always happen when they had an audience? He pulled back, not because he wanted to, but because she deserved more than to be mauled on a park bench. The thought was a fierce reminder. *She deserved more*. More than him. More than a man who'd done the things he'd done. Who couldn't love her the way she deserved to be loved.

Because there was no way he could. His wife was gone. He knew that. It wasn't even about still being in love with Vicki. But Warrick could never let himself love the way he'd loved Vicki again. That just couldn't happen. Letting someone down when you loved them the way he'd loved Vicki...seeing what that did to a person to let them down in that way. He couldn't go through that again.

"I'm sorry," he said. He cursed under his breath and looked out at the fountain in the center of the park as he worked to get himself under control. The apology spoke more to the fact that he was sorry he couldn't be what she needed, but he knew it would sound like he was just apologizing for getting carried away in the moment. That was fine. Better she think that than go into the truth and have to explain why he wasn't—never could be—good enough for her.

He hated the way she shrugged like it was nothing and turned away from him. She picked up her soda and drank and then talked, filling the silence as he sat there calling himself every name he could think of. Every name for idiot and asshole he could dream up. He watched as she brushed it off like it was nothing, just as she always did, but he'd begun to be able to see through the mantle of toughness she often wore. And it made him hate himself all the more.

* * *

Tyvek watched the couple, his heart cracking again. She was with him. Warrick had lured her in again. He had to be trying to use her to trap Tyvek.

He'd thought she was smarter this time. That she'd

learned and wouldn't be so easy to entice now that she'd seen where loving him had gotten her. The truth was, she'd just never been strong enough to resist him. Try as he might, Tyvek had never been able to make Vicki see that Warrick Staunton was wrong for her. To make her strong enough to open her eyes and see the truth before her.

A tear fell as he watched and he swiped at it, letting anger creep up to burn out the pain. Anger and rage to cleanse and stop the heartache. If he didn't let the rage take over, he wouldn't survive watching her go down this path. Not again. Not this time. This time, things would be different.

CHAPTER 13

SARA SWITCHED the phone to her other shoulder before picking up a wooden spoon to stir the pasta she was cooking. "Yes," she sighed, "it was an amazing kiss." She was underselling the kiss. There was really no way to explain the things that man had done to her with his mouth. How his arms had felt around her. How her body had responded when he'd pulled her flush against him.

She dropped the spoon, jumping back as hot water splashed.

"I can't believe you waited to call me." Samantha said on the other end of the line. "You should have called me the minute it happened."

"Oh, that wouldn't have been awkward at all. *Can you hang on a sec while I call a friend and tell her you kissed me brainless, Warrick? She'll want to know all about this kiss.* Yeah, that's not awkward or weird at all."

Samantha laughed. "You know what I mean."

"Mm hmm, I do." Sara turned the stove down and pulled the pasta off the burner. She needed to strain it, but she didn't have her prosthesis on. Straining pasta was best done with her robotic hand attached. She'd lost her enthusiasm for a meal, anyway. Her stomach had been in knots for the last day. Ever since *the kiss*.

"Brainless, huh?"

"Brain. Less. Completely brainless."

"Sooo, are you going to sleep with him?" Samantha was always direct.

"No! Are you kidding me? No."

"I thought maybe you'd changed your mind." Samantha sounded like she planned to try to make that change happen if it hadn't happened already. Most likely, she did.

Sara didn't answer as she padded to the living room and curled up on the couch. She'd fantasized about changing her mind but that was a long way off from going through with it. Being intimate just wasn't something she was ready for. She had guts. She always had. But the thought of being with a man terrified the crap out of her.

"Let me ask you something," Samantha said when she didn't get a response. "Does Warrick ever make you feel unsure?"

As soon as Samantha asked the question, the answer popped into Sara's head. She didn't even have to think about it. The answer was no. Even when he'd pulled back from the kiss the day before, she'd had the sense it was about him. About the fact that he wasn't ready to be with someone yet. She knew his wife's death had hit him hard. There was no denying that. For whatever reason, he wasn't moving on. And she respected that. It didn't have anything to do with her or his level of attraction to her. It hadn't been about her hand.

She'd done her best to brush off the kiss and continue as if nothing had happened. She knew if she were in his place, it was what she would want. She wouldn't want someone making a big deal of things. But Samantha's question made her realize, he hadn't made her feel uneasy in the way Samantha was asking. She hadn't felt rejected as a woman, the way she had when her fiancé had left her. She hadn't felt unwanted and damaged.

"Well?" Samantha pressed. Sara could tell Samantha wouldn't let go of this. Her directness had always been something Sara liked.

"No. He doesn't make me feel bad at all." She rushed to qualify that. "But that doesn't mean I'm ready for anything to happen." Just talking about Warrick gave her that fluttery stomach feeling she knew came with a new relationship. She had to remind herself, it wasn't a relationship with him. Letting herself fall into the trap of thinking anything else would be dangerous. It would lead to hurt.

"That's okay. But you can still let yourself live a little. You can practice being around a man again and feeling good about that. I have a feeling Warrick will be very good practice for you."

"So, what, we'd just be friends who kiss sometimes? And practice hanging out together?" Could it really be that simple?

"Why not?" Samantha sounded so breezy and light, Sara found herself wondering the very same thing. Why not?

CHAPTER 14

"I NEED PRACTICE." Sara realized how stupid the words sounded the minute they left her mouth, but the damage was done. She stood in the doorway to Warrick's office. It occurred to her she'd spent a lot of energy trying to avoid his office. She seemed to be doing a crap job of that one lately.

Warrick looked up at her. "You do?" He'd undone his tie, leaving it hanging loosely around his neck. The effect was ridiculously hot. She had to refocus before she lost her nerve.

"Yes."

"Okay." He looked at her, but didn't say more, and she realized she was going to need to spell it out.

"Just, you know. I mean...." She waved her hand in the air as though that might magically make him understand. "Just you know, hanging out. And like, well, like you know."

"Do I?" He quirked a brow. The man shouldn't be so sexy. Hand to God, it was just not fair.

"Yes. You do." She folded her arms and leveled him with a look of her own. He knew damned well what she meant. And, no, she wouldn't spell it out for him.

He answered her with a laugh. "I do. I just wanted to hear you say it."

"No sex." She blurted this little tidbit out then wanted to crawl under a table or behind a chair or something. She could feel the heat in her cheeks and swore under her breath. She was a veteran for crying out loud. She didn't *blush*.

"So, not a date?"

She raised her chin a hair, refusing to give him the satisfaction of seeing her squirm. Really, on the inside, there was a hell of a lot of squirming going on. "No. Not a date. No sex. Maybe kissing. But no sex."

He gave her a long look but she forced herself to stand still when she really wanted to turn and run. She held her ground while he watched her.

The next words that came out of his mouth shocked the hell out of her and took away any hope she'd had of doing this without squirming.

His voice was deep and sexy in that octave that said he was thinking about taking her clothes off. "I'm not sure I can do that, Sara."

She inhaled slowly, then nodded. Did that mean what she thought it meant? Technically, he'd said no. Sort of. But he'd said it in a way that seemed to say he wanted to put his hands on her. The memory of those hands on her came flying back and she was sure now she was flushed. And squirming. She nodded again and turned way, high tailing it back to her own office where things were safe. Where she didn't feel like she'd just flung herself out of a plane with a doily and some duct tape for a chute.

An hour later, she sat staring at her computer screen, still replaying the scene in her head. She'd really, really wanted that to go differently.

A knock on the door had her looking up. Carl, the teenager who worked in the mailroom three afternoons a week, didn't take his headphones off as he handed her an interoffice envelope. She took the envelope, waiting until he'd left to open it.

A single sheet of paper with a handwritten note. *Saturday. 7 pm. Not a date.*

CHAPTER 15

DINNERS with his mother were never fun. Warrick's mother insisted on having them served by her staff in the formal dining room rather than just sitting down for a meal as a normal family might. Then again, they weren't normal. His mother had never cooked like other mothers did.

Jonathan entered now, late in the way he usually was.

Warrick felt the immediate kick of the betrayal in his gut that seemed to always come with his uncle now. He shoved it aside and reminded himself Jonathan had never meant to hurt him. That he'd had no way to see what William Tyvek would do with the information Jonathan gave him. He was making a conscious effort to salvage the relationship he had with the last of his family.

"Sorry, sorry. I got caught up." Jonathan kissed Warrick's mother on the cheek. "How are you, sis?" Warrick smothered a smile. His mother most certainly never acted like anyone's "sis". She believed in formality and station in life. She hated when Jonathan called her that. But, like a kid who'd figured out what needled his older sister, Jonathan persisted in the game.

"What did you get caught up in?" Warrick asked, leaning back in his chair as one of the staff set a plate in front of him. There was a time when he knew all his mother and father's staff. His mother had become even more difficult to live with after his father's death, and most of the staff turned over with some regularity now. "Thank you," he murmured and lifted his fork and knife.

"That lovely woman Sara was showing me some of the devices she's been working on."

Warrick smiled and an immediate argument began in his head. He wasn't smiling at the mere mention of Sara. He was smiling at his uncle's excitement for her prostheses.

Fuck, that was a lie. He found himself grinning like an ass every time he even thought about her, never mind when she actually entered a room. She had that effect on him.

"I have to figure out where to take her Saturday," he said almost absently.

"Take her?" Jonathan asked.

"Who is Sara?" His mother interjected. "Why are we talking about some stranger I know nothing about at my dinner table?"

Warrick sighed. "She works at Simms." He frowned. "Well, actually she's a consultant of sorts. She's the woman who designed the prosthetic arms we're going to be manufacturing."

"What on earth would she want to do that for? Why would a woman want to design prosthetic anything?" His mother had put down her fork as though the very thought was distasteful. She didn't exactly live an enlightened life.

Warrick wished he drank alcohol more than once a year. He'd often thought alcohol might help him get through these biweekly meals at his mother's house, but he also knew if he began he would never stop. "I'd imagine it has to do with the fact she lost her hand serving in the military overseas."

Warrick could have predicted the eye roll from his mother. "What kind of woman does that? Women don't belong in the Army." To his mother, all military branches were referred to as the "Army."

"An honorable, brave intelligent one, that's who," Jonathan said before Warrick could speak. What Jonathan had said was true, though. Sara was all of that and more.

"She began by making a prosthetic that better suited her needs. She did it in her apartment with a simple 3D printing machine. When she realized the difference having a robotic hand could make in the life of an amputee, she set out to design one that was as functional as the high tech expensive models on the market without the high tech price tag."

"Her design is quite ingenious," Jonathan added.

Warrick nodded.

Jonathan flinched at her next words, as though the jab were personal, and Warrick knew why. The guilt was still there for Jonathan.

"Don't you have more important things to focus on, Warrick? Like saving my grandfather's company. When we handed you the reigns a decade ago, no one expected you to run it into the ground." She lifted her wine glass and drained it for the second time since they'd sat down to eat. It was immediately refilled by one of the staff.

Warrick was suddenly struck by the ridiculousness of the situation. When his father had been alive, they'd had Francine, who despite her soft name ran the kitchen and mealtime with an iron fist. When his mother began to chug whatever drink of choice she was on that month, Francine would purposefully dawdle in between filling her glass.

Warrick would never forget the time he'd realized why Francine hadn't been fired. He'd been too naïve to see the dynamic for what it was. It had taken walking in on his father and Francine in the study one day.

He'd pieced things together after that. Suffice it to say, his father appeared to have certain needs in the bedroom his mother wasn't willing to fulfill. When her husband had died, his mother had lost it, firing Francine and kicking her out of the house within days. The look on Francine's face was haunting. Warrick had always had the odd sense that Francine loved both his father and his mother. That somehow, she'd been part of their relationship in a way he would never understand himself. But what did he know about healthy relationships?

Nothing. He'd demonstrated that when he'd failed Vicki over and over.

"Warrick is doing a fine job focusing on the company and its return to the respect it deserves. In fact, Sara is an integral part of that. The goodwill her project is already sparking in the community is bringing invaluable PR that will soon have people forgetting what happened with Tyvek."

Warrick drew himself back to the conversation as his uncle attempted to defend him. It was useless. His mother would see what she wanted to see. He spoke to his uncle rather than his mother. "Carrie is arranging for us to use the clinic at the shelter to match veterans who need a prosthesis. We'll be able to do the screening, measuring, fitting and training with them there. Sara said that a lot of times, people need to return to see the prosthetist frequently, especially in the beginning to be sure the fit is adjusted properly. Carrie's agreed to spearhead that part of things for us."

"That should bring some good PR for the shelter as

well, help them recover from this," Jonathan said. "How is Carrie? Is she past that infection?"

Warrick nodded, pushing his plate away. "Yes. She was back at work when I talked to her and said she'd been cleared to return full time."

"Good," Jonathan nodded, pushing his own plate away. Warrick's mother continued to eat, having cut her meat into minuscule bites, as was her habit. Jonathan and Warrick were used to having to wait for her to finish. "That's good. So, you're taking Sara out? Where do you think you'll take her?"

"I don't know. It's not a date, so I'm steering clear of anything that feels like a date."

"Ah. That limits things a bit when a single man and a single woman go out," Jonathan said.

Warrick's mother broke her silence again. "So, that's your plan? You'll be giving away product to try to buy Simms Pharmaceutical's way back into the good graces of the doctors and patients?" She snorted an inelegant snort. "You'd think you would have learned a thing or two from your grandfather. Even your father-in-law could have taught you a great deal about business. You should have listened to him a bit more."

Warrick turned his head slowly, stunned she'd talk about William Tyvek like he was some great businessman instead of the maniac they'd now discovered him to be. Yes, he'd been great at business, but he'd also been a highly successful murderer. Warrick's conversation with Jarrod came back to him and he stilled, looking at his mother.

"What?" She barked.

He shook his head. "Nothing. Nothing at all. Jonathan, I'll see you during the week. Maybe we can get lunch." For now, he needed to place a call to Jarrod Harmon. He might have been wrong about his mother's willingness to help Tyvek.

Jonathan gave his sister a weary look that said he was tired of the theatrics she seemed to crave. As tired of them as Warrick was. He offered a weak smile for Warrick and nodded. "Next week."

Warrick turned to walk away, but Jonathan called out to him. "Warrick, try the museum. It makes a nice place for a not-date date."

CHAPTER 16

"HAVE you ever been to the Yale Collection of Musical Instruments?" Warrick asked as he opened the passenger door to his car for Sara. She eyed the car as though she wasn't entirely comfortable sitting on luxury leather seats, then slipped in. He saw the glint in her eye when she felt the softness of the seats envelop her. It was something he'd grown up taking for granted. He knew now how lucky he was to have luxuries in his life. In fact, he'd been thinking he might downgrade his car a bit. The Maybach he'd been in for the last two years was a luxury not a necessity.

"No," Sara said, after he'd shut her door and jogged around to his own. "What is it?"

"It's a museum. Yale houses a gorgeous collection of old instruments. Everything from harpsichords to string and percussion instruments from around the world. It's not well-known, but it's beautiful. I thought maybe we'd head there, then grab a bite to eat on the green."

Sara turned to smile at him as he pulled onto the highway, and his groin kicked into high speed just as the car did.

It was going to be a long night if his body kept responding to her like that.

"Sounds great." She turned back to look out the front of the car.

"I used to love it when I was in school. I'd go there sometimes just to get away from things. The collection doesn't change very much, but I'd always manage to find something new to look at."

"You went to Yale?"

He nodded. "It was expected. It's the family school." He frowned. "Sorry, that sounded stuck up. It's just that there was never any question that's where I'd go. If I hadn't gotten in, my father would have paid my way in. Or, at least, that was his plan. I'm not sure that really goes on anymore."

Now she was watching him again, and he focused on pulling into a spot a block away from Prague Hall where the music school was housed.

"You would have hated that, wouldn't you?" She asked quietly.

"What? Having my dad buy a spot for me?" He laughed. "Oh yeah. In fact, that was more motivation for me to get in than anything else. I don't know why, but it didn't occur to me to rebel and go someplace else. I wanted to sail in on my merits so he wouldn't get the satisfaction of making some grand donation to save me."

They got out of the car and he hit the key fob to lock the doors as he gestured across the street. She was quiet as they walked across the street and into the Yale campus through one of the old stone walkways that would take them to the right building. He had to admit, the campus was stunning. There'd always been a sense of reverence about the buildings for him. Like he could somehow hear the voices of the past speak to him there.

"You and your dad didn't get along?"

"No. Not at all." He took her hand in his and led them to the right, matching her shorter strides. "But who does?"

She didn't say anything and he didn't know if she was simply giving him the chance to expand or if she got along with her dad and didn't understand what he was talking about.

"Sorry, I don't mean to bitch and moan about my childhood. Believe me, I know I had it easy. I wasn't abused, always had money and a roof over my head, and had advantages I can't even begin to count. Let's just say, my dad and I didn't agree on anything. That translated into motivation to show him up. To be better than him. To take over the company he had no interest in running, and to build it into something even bigger and better than it was."

"Did he get into Yale?" She asked with a grin.

"Of course he did. There was a large donation made that year by my grandfather. And every year after that for five years."

"Five?"

Warrick shrugged. "He wasn't the best student." He opened the door to the collection and paid their entry fee.

"So did your dad run the company before you?"

"No, he never had any interest in it. My dad liked to party and travel and spend money. He wasn't really into working. Luckily, my grandfather was happy running the company until I took over."

"Is he still alive?"

"No. He died six years ago."

"I'm sorry," she said, quietly. She didn't say what he had a feeling she was thinking. He'd lost his grandfather six years ago, his father four, and his wife three.

He nodded, never sure what to say when people offered their condolences for a loss like that.

She seemed content to let it go.

Together, they entered the first of the exhibit halls. He heard the intake of her breath at the sight. He'd reacted much the same way when he'd first seen the exhibit.

He was partial to the harpsichord room himself and they moved in that direction. He watched her face as she took in the harpsichords of every shape and size, some with polished shining wood, others with murals or decorative edgings painted on them.

"Oh, wow. These are incredible." The hushed tone in her voice was one he understood. They were incredible. The collection ranged in color, shape, and size. Some were plain in decoration, but even those had a burnished shine to their wood and decades of nicks and wear that spoke of their secret history. Others were hand painted masterpieces where the art itself was worthy of collection.

He noticed right away, though, that Sara seemed to view them differently.

The realization ran through him, warming his chest. She was so different. It was what made her so enticing. She bent and studied the inner workings of one of the instruments, then bent further. Christ, she was getting to him, and he could honestly say it wasn't just the sight of her pants pulling tight over her backside and the view she was giving him. Although, if he were honest that was doing things to him that he probably wouldn't be able to ignore much longer.

It was how she saw the world. He liked watching her face as she studied the instruments.

"They're amazing." She moved to the next, then

another next to that, a piece that held two keyboards, one on top of the other.

She was equally fascinated with the other instruments in the collection, her face lighting at the smallest of percussion instruments or the largest horn. It hadn't occurred to him that she would value and appreciate how each piece worked so much, but it should have. She was an engineer. She saw things in ways he and others didn't, and that was quickly becoming one of his favorite things about her.

Sara wished she could say she had a bad time, but she hadn't. After visiting the Yale collection, they'd grabbed pizza, then wandered around the rest of the campus looking at the old buildings. She hadn't taken the time to walk the campus before, and she had to admit, it was gorgeous.

Now, sitting in Warrick's car as he pulled into her building's parking lot, she suddenly felt nervous. The kind of jangly nerves that tell you something is about to happen. She could feel the shift in the air as Warrick came around and opened her car door, offering a hand to her as they walked into the building.

Before they reached the entrance, he broke the silence. "Why do you need this practice, Sara?" She knew he was referring to practice being around a man again. Dating.

She let out a breath and decided telling him was better than trying to skirt around the issue. She'd never really been one to skirt. "My fiancé left me right after I was injured. Said he couldn't handle it." She raised her prosthesis and made the muscle movement in her forearm that caused the robotic fingers to wave.

Warrick didn't comment but raised his brows and she

could see in the stark shadow in his eyes that he had some thoughts on the subject.

"I guess, since then, I have friends and my family, but I don't date. I'm careful to keep things from going there. I've been sort of hiding out from that side of things. Hiding out from life in some ways."

"I have some experience with that." They stopped in front of her apartment and he turned her to face him. Her breath caught at his intense expression. "You said we could practice this part a little."

"Okay," she murmured, and realized almost immediately, it was too husky, too breathless.

He leaned closer and heaven help her, she pressed into him, lifting onto her toes slightly as he came down to meet her. His mouth closed on hers and the jangly nerves flipped into overdrive.

The kiss was hot and hard and soft all at once. It wasn't the kind of kiss that only happened with your mouth. It was a whole body kiss, his arms coming around her to pull her close. And damn, if her body didn't just sit up and beg for more. A lot more.

He softened the kiss, letting his lips barely brush over hers for a moment, before deepening it once again, as if going back for seconds. Sara brought her right hand up to his shoulder, running it over the muscles and letting herself sink into the feel of his body wrapped around hers. It was a feeling she had missed. One she wasn't sure she'd ever experience again.

Then he pulled back and broke the kiss, and she realized with a start she hadn't been ready for it to end yet. He studied her for a minute, and she saw the smallest of smiles form. "Good night, Sara."

And then he was gone.

CHAPTER 17

WARRICK TOSSED his keys on the side table in his entranceway and stalked to the kitchen. Kissing Sara had felt entirely too good. He'd meant for it to be a quick kiss goodnight, but it had gotten out of hand much too quickly. He'd been seconds away from hauling her inside her apartment and stripping her bare. Stripping her and exploring every inch of her. Seeing what she liked and didn't like. Finding out what made her moan. What made her come.

And that couldn't happen. It couldn't. It wasn't fair to Sara.

He grabbed a bottle of water and chugged half of it, then realized water wasn't going to cool him down. Drinking it wouldn't, anyway. It would take a lot more than that to stop what Sara had started.

He turned, planning to take a cold shower, but caught sight of the rose bush he'd transplanted from the old house. The sight of its yellowing leaves was enough to douse the heat, at least partially.

It sat outside the sliding door leading to his patio. He moved closer and saw that a lot of the leaves had a yellow tinge to them and a few of the branches looked funny. They were darker and looked like they were collapsing on themselves somehow. Maybe they were dry.

He went to the kitchen for the watering can, giving the plant a good drink of water. Maybe he hadn't been watering it enough.

Walking into his bedroom and kicking off his shoes, he pulled up the web browser on his phone. He didn't know what to search for. *Save a rose bush.* The search pulled up all kinds of results, and the memory of the kiss with Sara was nothing more than that; a memory that tickled at the back of his mind as he read through the results of his search.

He would fix this. He needed to fix this.

CHAPTER 18

DETECTIVE JARROD HARMON hung up the phone, knowing without looking at his partner that he was sporting a dumbass grin a mile wide. Carrie Hastings had taken his breath away the first time he saw her. He still loved it when she called in the middle of the day to see how his day was going. It was no wonder she owned his heart.

His partner, Cal Rylan, seemed about ready to open his mouth to comment when Jarrod's phone rang again. He gave Cal a look designed to tell him to shut up and drive, then smiled wider and answered. They were headed to have a chat with Warrick Staunton's mother and see if she had any information about William Tyvek's whereabouts.

"Detective Harmon." He listened for a few minutes, asked a few questions, then hung up. After months of searching, this was the first lead they'd had on Tyvek, but as leads went, it was shit.

"The lab?" Cal asked, likely having guessed from the questions Jarrod had asked.

"Yeah. Get this. There was a break-in reported the day William Tyvek slipped out of that fire." He didn't need to specify that it was the fire Tyvek had set and left Carrie in to make it look like Warrick Staunton had killed her. Cal had been there. He knew Tyvek was insane. Knew he'd slipped into the ether somehow after almost taking Carrie from Jarrod.

If that had happened, Jarrod didn't know how he would have survived it. Before he'd met Carrie, he knew he was missing something in his life. He'd even had a vague idea that finding the right woman might be the answer to that missing piece. He'd never in a million years guessed how much of a difference finding the woman you were meant to spend a lifetime with would make. She was…well, she was simply everything to him. There was no other way to put it.

"Yeah? What the hell does a break-in have to do with Tyvek? They find a link?"

Jarrod nodded. "Not much was missing from the house. Clothing and food. It looked like the perp had broken in primarily to bandage wounds from some kind of injury. The CSI guys collected blood samples from the scene and lifted a few prints, but the samples have been sitting on the shelf while higher priority stuff was processed. No one really thought the case would go anyplace. Even the homeowners didn't press the issue. They had wanted the report on file in case they discovered something else missing or the person came back."

"Tyvek?" Cal asked, his face telling Jarrod he was just as surprised as he'd been. It was a random lead, and not one he thought would have been found.

"Uh huh. Prints match. They only lifted prints from the box the bandages were held in. They figured it wasn't worth dusting the whole place. In fact, the only reason they collected anything at all was because they had a rookie on scene that day and wanted him to practice. We don't have a

DNA sample from Tyvek to compare the blood, but it's reasonable to think Tyvek was there alone and injured."

Cal squinted his eyes in thought. "Can they tell us anything about the injury? Was he burned in the fire or maybe injured getting away?"

Jarrod shook his head. "She said she can't tell. She did say she might theorize if there was a burn wound, there might be more dead skin on the bandages. They only found blood. But she said that was just theory and she really had no way of knowing."

"Doesn't give us much," Cal said, giving voice to Jarrod's thoughts, "but at least we have another stop on his trail."

Jarrod lifted his phone. "I'll call tech and see if they can check traffic cameras in the area for him. Maybe we'll get lucky and find another piece to the puzzle."

Cal nodded. "We can canvas the area, see if anyone remembers seeing him. Check for reports of stolen vehicles in that area. How far was it from the fire?"

"Not far at all. Less than a mile."

Jarrod stopped relaying the report to Cal long enough to tell the tech team what he needed, then hung up. "They're going to check for other break-ins during that time frame, too."

"I've always assumed he used his money and influence to leave the country, or at least the area. He's the last person I would have guessed would be breaking into houses to patch himself up."

Jarrod rubbed the back of his neck. At least they had something to go on now. It was thin as hell and didn't give them much, but it was the first credible lead they'd had in weeks.

CHAPTER 19

THE WOMAN GAVE THEM NOTHING.

Warrick had warned them his mother was a bit stiff and formal, but he hadn't known it would be this bad. After being shown to a sitting room by a uniformed housekeeper, they'd been made to wait twenty minutes for Anna Elizabeth Simms Staunton to appear.

Jarrod cringed at the name. Somehow, it screamed privilege and money. It also seemed a bit much. Who went by that many names? He wondered if she signed all four names when she wrote a check or signed a form.

Warrick's mother had been, well, dramatic was probably the best word for it. Or perhaps theatrical. Whatever the word, she thrived on attention and confrontation. Jarrod couldn't imagine the parenting tactics the woman would employ. Must have been a hell of an upbringing.

"I'm sure I don't know what you're talking about. Why would I have any continued contact with William Tyvek?" Anna Elizabeth placed a splayed hand on her breast as though she needed to hold onto her heart from the shock of their questions. Like it might get up and run right out of her chest cavity.

He and Cal were there simply because Warrick had gotten the uncomfortable feeling his mom might have been involved in hiding Tyvek. Warrick hadn't had anything to back that feeling, but if a guy calls and asks you to look into his mom's involvement in a crime, well, that tended to get them to sit up and notice. Not to mention, they needed more to go on in this case.

Warrick had asked Jarrod not to mention he'd been the one to instigate this chat. Jarrod was going to do all he could to respect Warrick's wishes. The man had lost enough throughout this ordeal. His mother might be a piece of work, but she was the man's mother. That had to count for something.

"We're simply asking if you have any information on where he might be hiding." Cal answered calmly and Jarrod knew his partner was looking for any telltale sign. Any flinch or crack in her demeanor.

He had to give her credit. She maintained her composure. She'd moved on from the hand to her heart thing and had picked up her teacup, holding the miniature plate that went with it in one hand.

"Why would I have any information about where he is?" She was the picture of innocence. In fact, too much so.

Jarrod noticed she had yet to deny having any information. She continued to turn their questions around, deflecting without flat-out denying. The tactic was one they'd seen when someone didn't want to be straight. It also told him she had a lot of practice at this. She was a skilled and experienced manipulator.

"Your families spent a lot of time together while your kids were growing up, didn't they? I understand you have houses down at the Cape near one another? And his daughter was married to your son. He's family, in a sense."

She made a face, but Jarrod couldn't decipher the meaning behind it. They'd had the police on Cape Cod check Tyvek's house repeatedly over the last couple of months, but they'd called and asked them to keep an eye on the Staunton's Cape house as well. So far, they'd reported there was no activity.

A glance at his partner told him Cal thought something was off about her behavior as well.

They tried the whole spiel about aiding and abetting, but she didn't crack. Twenty minutes later, as they walked out, Jarrod wasn't one hundred percent satisfied she didn't know more, but it was hard to tell. From what Warrick had told her, she might get off on them thinking she knew more when in fact she didn't. Either way, his frustration level was hitting all-time highs with this hunt. They were no closer to Tyvek now than they'd been all month. Getting justice for Carrie and all the people Tyvek had killed seemed to be slipping away, and there was no way Jarrod was going to let that happen.

CHAPTER 20

"WE SHOULD PRACTICE your everyday guy skills tonight." Sara had to hold back a laugh at the look on Warrick's face. She'd shown up around lunchtime, knowing he'd still be deep in his work, but Charlotte would be away from her desk.

"My what now?" He did that sexy thing where the corners of his mouth twitched and she knew he was holding back a smile. It had become a challenge to see if she could make him laugh or smile. Both were equally rewarding. The smile was often cocky with a promise behind it that said he could do wicked things to a woman. The laugh was low and it always made her body warm in response.

She moved into the office and sat across from him, her face sobering as she thought about how to frame this conversation. She went with direct. "You're leaving after this, aren't you?"

Now his face lost its humor. "What?"

"After you bring the company back. You're leaving. I can tell. You've got that half packed and out the door look about you." She tried to sound casual as she said it, but she wasn't feeling casual on the inside. She felt tense and had that itchy sense she'd always gotten overseas when she knew there was a problem with something but didn't know how to fix things before everything went sideways on her or her team.

He was quiet a minute, then nodded. She had to shove aside the feelings of disappointment that swamped her. It was foolish to feel anything in response to him leaving. She had no claim on him. So they'd hung out? Kissed? They'd said at the start it was nothing more than a friendship.

Then why did the thought of him leaving hurt? She forced a smile. "You'll be like one of those wild baby eagles they rescue with a hurt wing or something. They can rehab them but then they can't let them loose in the world because they have no idea how to catch food."

That brought the humor back, along with a bark of laughter from him. And, damn, there was that freaking heat. "I can't believe you just compared me to a bird. Do I have to eat mice in this little scenario of yours because I gotta tell you, I draw the line at eating mice."

She found herself laughing too and was glad there wasn't the awkward tension between them she'd feared would be there after the way he'd kissed her the other night. "No. You know what I mean. You have no idea how to be a normal guy. Think about it. You won't be the great heir to the Simms Empire or the CEO of a company. You'll just be a normal guy."

"You're probably right. I have no idea how to do that." He leaned back in his seat. "I suppose you have some strategy to fix this?"

"Uh huh." She grinned and held up the tickets she'd bought. "Hockey."

* * *

Warrick handed a beer to Sara and took the seat next to her as the Wolf Pack mascot began shooting T-shirts into the stands.

"It always amazes me that someone had invented a gun dedicated to shooting T-shirts." She nodded toward the mascot.

"Proves there's a market for everything. If you can make it, there's someone, someplace that wants to buy it."

She looked at him. "You really think that?" She shook her head at him. "Nah I don't buy it. You're a numbers guy. I've seen you cut projects that needed to be cut. If the numbers aren't there, you pull the plug."

He shrugged. "I didn't say it would be a good market. You might only sell one of what you make, but I think there's someone out there who wants even the worst inventions. I think a lot of inventions fail because they can't bring the product to the right people. The right market."

She shook her head, but he didn't know what she was thinking. He liked that about her. She kept him on his toes. She could surprise him and that was refreshing in a woman. He put one arm around the back of her chair and leaned back, taking a drink of the beer.

"You're getting good at this." She smiled as she said it and he leaned in and kissed her mouth. He couldn't resist. He'd been wanting to do it the whole ride up to Hartford.

"Good at what?" He said after he pulled away. He liked the slightly dazed look in her eyes. He liked that he could put that look there.

"At, um..." She licked her lips and he focused on them again. How could he help it? "At relaxing like a normal guy."

He turned to the ice, feeling better than he'd felt in a long time. "Who are we rooting for?"

That made her sit up and gawk at him, and he had to laugh at the look on her face.

"The Wolf Pack, of course!" She looked around as though checking to be sure no one had overheard him and he laughed.

"We can't pull for the away team?" now he was just teasing her, but she made it fun.

"No! Are you crazy?"

"Apparently." He took a sip of the beer, then couldn't resist. "But I like the..." He looked up at the scoreboard to see who the Wolf Pack was playing and she called him on it.

"You don't even know who they're playing!"

"Nope. Clearly, I need more practice at this." The more practice, the better, he thought. If it involved spending time with Sara, he was all in.

CHAPTER 21

WARRICK LOOKED up at the knock on his office door. "Hey, Uncle Jonathan." He stilled at the look on his uncle's face. "What is it?"

Jonathan came in and shut the door. "I just had a visit from three of the cousins." That's what they'd always called them: *the cousins*. Warrick wasn't completely sure when or how it had started, but it had stuck into adulthood.

He tossed his pen on the desk. "Let me guess. Jacob, Gus, and Mara?"

Jonathan shook his head. "Almost got it. Jacob, Gus, and Vincent."

Warrick cursed under his breath. Vincent had been one of the less aggressive of the bunch. If they'd gotten him on board, things were getting worse.

"What did they want?"

"They wanted my vote to replace you. Naturally, they didn't get it."

Warrick let out a breath. He hadn't been one hundred percent sure of Jonathan's loyalty and the rush of relief hit him hard. When Jonathan had taken their drug formula to

William Tyvek, a fissure had formed in the tight bond they'd had. It had been healing over the past few weeks, but hearing that Jonathan hadn't hesitated in sticking with him against the cousins went a long way toward cementing the patch.

"Did they say who they wanted to replace me with?"

Before Jonathan could answer, Charlotte interrupted on the intercom. "Warrick, Jack Sutton is on the phone. He wants to know if he can come see you. He says he's five minutes away."

Warrick's gaze met his uncle's and he held it as he answered her. "Yes, tell him to come over. And, Charlotte, send him in when he gets here, please." He turned and sent an email moving an appointment to another day, then looked back at his uncle. "I bet they went to Sutton after you said no. They might be hoping if they convinced him, you'd come on board and they could pull together enough votes that way."

Jonathan nodded. "They want to bring in Myles Carson from Innovennux."

Warrick stood and went to the window. Myles Carson had saved Innovennux when he'd gone there four years ago, but he'd done it by splitting off three of the company's technologies and selling them to the highest bidders. He'd sacrificed employee jobs when the buyers wanted to bring their own staff. Every move the man had made put dollars above people. Every damned time. It wasn't at all what Warrick's grandfather had taught him to do. It wasn't what Simms was about.

"Even if they get Jack on board, they won't have enough stock for a majority."

Warrick didn't turn around. "They will if they convince mother to side with them."

"Oh, surely she wouldn't do that." Jonathan didn't sound any more convinced than Warrick was. His mother was unpredictable. He'd like to say she'd defend him, but honestly, he couldn't say that with any certainty.

He stared out at nothing as he waited for Jack to arrive. Five minutes dragged on, but when the door opened, Jack's eyes went from Jonathan's face to Warrick's and back again.

Warrick waited. He could see Jack struggling with whether to speak in front of Jonathan.

"If it's all right with you, Jack, I'd like Jonathan to stay for this," Warrick said. He meant it. He wanted to stand shoulder to shoulder with Jonathan in saving the company now. He only hoped they could do it.

Jack nodded. "Jonathan, I'm guessing they came to you first?" He strode across the room and stood across from both men. "I trust you said no?"

The breath whooshed out of Warrick. "Does this mean you're not siding with them?" He didn't need to tell Jack who *them* was.

The look Jack gave Warrick was almost comical. "No. Hell, no. I just wanted to be sure we had Jonathan with us so they can't pull anything behind our backs. I thought we might need to convince him. I'm behind you, Warrick. One hundred percent."

Warrick put his hands to face and scrubbed. "Jesus, you couldn't tell me that over the phone?"

Jack shrugged and laughed. "I was nearby."

CHAPTER 22

SARA LOOKED at Warrick across the room, where he stood talking to the production guy. He seemed completely at ease surrounded by lights and cameras, as though being interviewed for a news piece was nothing. They hadn't gotten much warning about the appearance, but she'd been told that was the way these things often happened. The station needed a spot filled and they got a tip on a feel-good story and rolled with it. If you wanted the free publicity, you showed up. Even if the idea of it did make you want to puke.

"You'll be on in two minutes." The woman with the clipboard didn't look up as she spoke. She continued to read her notes and even broke periodically to speak into a walkie talkie on her hip. It was nerve-wracking, but the whole thing was nerve-wracking to Sara. She wasn't used to wearing makeup and having her hair all done up.

And honestly, her feelings about Warrick were only making it worse. She was all too aware of how her body was reacting to him. Of how her stomach did flip flops every time he looked at her across the room. He walked toward her now, eyes seeming to sweep over her. She wanted to sink through the floorboards. She probably had to admit at some point that this had gone past friendship. At least, for her, it had.

He came close, looking at her and she saw the slightest tilt to his mouth. He leaned in close, coming down to one ear. Damn if she didn't lean into him, her right hand coming up to meet his chest. It was like her body went into autopilot despite her objections.

We have objections? A little voice inside her head chimed in and the nerves cranked higher. Apparently, the voice didn't have objections.

"Sara, breathe." He whispered in her ear and she let out her breath in a whoosh, shocked to realize she'd been holding it. Then she found she couldn't suck another breath in, and she started to panic.

"Hey." He drew back and took hold of her arms, running his hands up and down. The sensation began to ground her. His words helped a lot, too. "Hey, you'll be fine. They're going to love you. All you have to do is talk to Marcus."

"Marcus?" She squeaked.

He nodded and she saw a smile quirk those lips. "Marcus Mahoney? You know, the guy who runs the show?"

"Oh, right. Right." The guy whose face was on billboards all over the city. The guy who was a local celebrity and news icon. *That* guy.

"Look at me."

Sara did just that. She turned her focus to Warrick. Her breathing steadied as she looked at his face. She kept her eyes on his.

Those hands of his kept going up and down her arms.

"Pretend you're just talking to Marcus as a friend out there. Don't worry about anything else. He's a nice guy. He won't bite, I promise."

She nodded and took a slow breath. Maybe she could do this. "Okay. A friend. Okay."

"You're on," the woman with the clipboard said in a tone that said she could give a rat's ass that Sara was in the middle of a breakdown.

"Sara, you got this." Warrick's voice held the confidence she'd had when she'd been in the military. When she'd had to make quick calls under pressure or face an open road with God knows what between her unit and their base. When she'd had to learn to live without her hand.

She snapped out of her panic. What was she doing? She *did* have this. She nodded again, squared her shoulders, threw a smile on her face and walked out to talk to Marcus Mahoney.

CHAPTER 23

"UM, this doesn't look like practicing to be a regular guy," Sara said, as Warrick pulled in front of the curb at a fancy restaurant. A valet opened her door, but she looked over at Warrick, instead of getting out.

The smile he gave her could have melted the panties off half the adult female population of New Haven. "It's not. Just trust me on this one. We're practicing something else tonight."

"Oh yeah?" She gave him the voice that said she wanted answers, even though her panties were busy packing their bags for their trip south. "What is that?"

He didn't fall for it. "I'll tell you later."

He got out of his now-open door and handed the valet his key, leaving Sara to turn to the man still holding her door. His look of patience told her how much this place cost.

"Thank you," she murmured, then looked down at herself. She'd forgotten she'd been dressed in a navy dress for the show, her hair and makeup still done. Samantha had brought Jill and Jennie and Kelly over to dress her, swearing they were responsible for all of Samantha's clothing choices. She'd trusted them, and was glad she had or she'd have felt even more awkward walking into a place like this.

Warrick took her hand and walked through the door, nodding to the host holding it for them.

"Good evening, Mr. Staunton." A smiling woman who looked like she might be either an owner or manager greeted them, then instructed a host to show them to their table. So, he'd either planned ahead and reserved a table, or they simply gave him one whenever he walked through the door. Neither would surprise her.

They ordered drinks and listened to the waiter talk about specials. Sara kept her left hand in her lap and fingered the menu with her right hand.

"What looks good to you?" Warrick asked.

"It all looks good." It was true. She'd seen four or five entrees already that sounded amazing. Her mouth watered at the descriptions and the restaurant was filled with heavenly smells.

"I've had the salmon, the chicken, and the prime rib. They're all amazing. The chef here probably couldn't mess anything up if he tried. My favorite thing is the red snapper, if you like fish."

It was one of the items she'd already flagged as possible. She set down her menu and nodded. "Done."

The waiter approached the table within seconds and Warrick ordered for both of them. He added a bowl of soup for himself. "Would you like a salad or soup, Sara?"

"Um..."

The waiter handed her back the menu. "I recommend the baby bibb with apples and blue cheese."

Sara nodded. "That sounds good, thank you."

A second waiter brought their drinks while a third

placed flatware next to their plates based on what they had ordered for dinner. She'd never seen so many wait staff serve one table. When they'd left, Warrick spoke first.

"You were great with Marcus. The interview was fantastic."

She laughed. "I have a few other words for it."

"Nah. You were great. You know, it was interesting when he asked if we'd be working on prosthetics for lower limbs. We could always see if Jax Cutter wants to work with you to design something. If you're interested, that is." He sipped his beer. "He might be able to pull together some people to consult on it."

"I hadn't thought of it until he asked. I'd definitely need to work with someone to figure out what's required. The differences between designing a hand and designing a leg would be substantial."

"How so?" Warrick asked, and she got the sense he actually cared about the answer.

"Well, to be honest, I'm sure I don't know enough to recognize what all of the differences will be. I know enough to know I need to know a lot more." She lifted the white wine she'd ordered and took a sip, realizing she'd just said the word "know" about five hundred fifty-two times in one sentence. Her nerves were getting to her. "With a hand, the issue is grip strength and small motor control. Dexterity, the ability to shift and move the hand, to close it in more than a simple grip. A leg needs to hold the weight of the body, move at the knee in a natural way, balance when standing still and while moving." She stopped to think. "I'm honestly not sure where I'd start."

He grinned. "But you're thinking about it now. I can see those wheels turning."

She couldn't help but smile back. She was thinking

about it. She'd love to see what was on the market and look for ways to either improve what was available, or make the existing technology available in a more affordable way.

"We should talk to Jax about it," Warrick said.

Their soup and salad arrived and Sara was glad she'd ordered it. She realized she'd forgotten to eat lunch. She'd been nervous about the interview, but Warrick had been right. As soon as the host got her out there, he'd started talking to her like they were old friends, and she'd been able to relax.

She had to force herself to slow down so she didn't seem like she'd never had a decent meal. "How can a salad be this good?" She asked.

"I have two theories." Warrick surprised her with his answer. "One, I've discovered everything here is insanely fresh. Chances are, that lettuce was in the ground this morning."

Sara shook her head. "It's winter. They couldn't have gotten it locally."

Warrick gave a head shake of his own, but his was accompanied by a smug grin. "Hydroponics. They use a local place for much of their produce, and it's produced year-round with hydroponic farming."

Sara should have guessed that, she realized. She'd kind of love to see how they did it. "So what's the second part of your theory?" Sara asked, before taking the last bite of her salad.

"The dressing."

"Agreed. I'm easy to impress after eating military food, but that dressing was amazing."

"The food was that bad in the military?"

She laughed. "Oh yeah. Well, not all the time. It depended a lot on where we were. For basic training, the food was awful. But, then, you're so damned exhausted all the time, you probably wouldn't taste the difference if it was good so it didn't matter all that much. It was enough to get something in your stomach before you fell into bed for four hours of sleep, or something to hold you over during a five-hour march."

Sara leaned back as the waiter took her plate and a waitress stepped in with their fish. "Twice, when I was waiting to be deployed, we were on air force bases. The air force had some amazing food. I have no idea why, but it was fantastic. Unfortunately, we were never there for very long."

She bit into her red snapper and moaned. Warrick took his own bite and grinned at her. "Told you so."

"You were right. It's amazing." She couldn't help but close her eyes as the fish all but melted in her mouth.

"Air Force good?" he asked with a laugh.

"Ha! Okay, so the air force food wasn't quite this good, but at the time it seemed like it. When we were deployed overseas, the food wasn't too bad, I guess. It was worse the bigger the unit. It seemed like the more mouths to be fed, the worse the food got, which I guess makes sense."

"It does."

They ate in silence for a few minutes, and Sara was glad he didn't ask more about her time overseas. It wasn't something she talked much about, but it occurred to her how much easier it was to talk about a single aspect of it, like the food, than when people said things like, "tell me what it was like." Warrick had never done that with her, and she liked it.

From there, they talked about things as varied as moonrocks and water lilies, though she still wasn't sure how those topics had surfaced. She told him about her brothers, who still protected her like she was fifteen anytime they got together. They lived in her hometown where her parents still were, so she only saw them on holidays. She talked to them every other week or more often, though.

"Sara, Warrick. How's the ankle?" Sara looked up to see Andrew and Jill smiling at them.

Warrick stood and shook hands with Andrew and then Jill. "It's much better. Back to normal, so you'll have to get used to the idea of me saying no to any more basketball games, even if it does mean you guys win when you stick the other team with me."

Jill turned to Andrew. "Really?" Her tone and the look on her face said it all and Sara laughed as Andrew shrugged sheepishly.

"Are you guys coming or going?" Warrick asked.

"Going." Andrew slid his arm around Jill's waist.

Now Jill looked sheepish. "It's the first night we've had a babysitter in a long time but I'm too exhausted and not really feeling well." She laid a hand on her stomach and Sara's eyes narrowed in on the woman. She hadn't realized it, but Jill was wearing a loose-fitting dress and when she ran her hand over the fabric, there was a small swell underneath.

Sara's eyes went wide and she stood, pulling Jill in for a hug. "Oh my gosh, are you really?"

Tears filled Jill's eyes as she nodded and Andrew beamed. "She cries at the drop of a hat nowadays."

"Fifteen weeks, today." Jill's excitement was plain. "We told family last week, but we've been waiting a little while to spread the news. You know." She shrugged and Sara did know. Jill and Andrew had tried to get pregnant for a long time before adopting twins.

"But how?" Sara asked, then laughed and raised her

hand. "Stop, Andrew. I know you're about to try to give me a birds and bees lecture."

They all laughed but Jill grinned at Sara. "He *does* know what you mean. And no one knows. The doctors didn't have a real answer for us, and we didn't care."

"And now it's time to get her home to bed," Andrew said. They said their goodbyes and the couple left as Sara and Warrick resettled into their seats.

"So, what did I miss there?" Warrick asked. "Why is it surprising they're having a baby? I thought they had two kids already."

"They do," Sara said. "But the twins are adopted. They didn't think Jill could get pregnant."

"Oh." Warrick grabbed his drink and took a swallow.

"You okay?" Sara asked, but Warrick only had time to nod before the waiter came to the table with a tray of desserts. Each one looked better than the last, and as he described them, Sara had to fight not to sigh in pleasure and order one of everything.

They split dessert, sharing a decadent flourless chocolate cake, something she'd always loved.

"So, when are you going to tell me what we were practicing tonight?" Sara asked after Warrick had signed the check.

He took both of her hands in his. Both her natural hand and her prosthesis, lifting them from where they'd sat on the table. "It was about this," he said.

"I don't get it."

He rubbed small circles over her right hand. "It was about you forgetting to put your prosthesis in your lap, or to use only your right hand unless you absolutely have to use both hands for something."

He let her puzzle over his statement as he stood, then

pulled her up beside him. She didn't say anything as they walked to the door of the restaurant, and she realized she didn't have to. He was right. She'd forgotten all about her hand with him. As the night went on, it simply hadn't been an issue. It was normally something that was right at the surface for her. She was always aware of it, aware of people's impressions of it, of how it looked, how it might get in the way.

She'd completely forgotten to worry about it at some point in the evening.

Warrick pulled her right hand toward him, leaning over the table to kiss it. He followed by pulling her prosthesis toward him, leaning to kiss that, too. "Thank you for trusting me enough to forget it," he said quietly, and she felt a thrill race through her at the low gruff tone.

She was speechless, which was something she'd never experienced before. He didn't wait for her reaction. He stood, pulled her chair out and led her out. She'd be lying if she said she wasn't walking maybe a tiny little bit on air.

* * *

Warrick walked Sara into her apartment building, but forced himself to stop outside her door. He wanted to take her inside. No, scratch that. He all but needed to take her inside. To get his hands on her, to taste and touch every inch of her. To hear her moan, to make her whimper with need. To fill her, bury himself inside her.

But there was still a part of him that knew he wasn't ready for that. People assumed he'd been so in love with Vicki that he mourned her to this day. His feelings for his wife were complicated. He was smart enough to realize there was a hell of a lot of guilt wrapped up in it. Yes, there was love. But the guilt was there, too. And that was a hell of a thing to get a handle on.

But then Sara looked at him and everything but her faded away. She unlocked her door, before turning to smile up at him. He reached for her. There wasn't any stopping it. Sara melted against him as he pulled her in to kiss her. His body roared to life in response. She did things to him he never thought any woman would again. He brought his hands to cup her face and turned to deepen the kiss, wanting to taste more of her. She tasted of wine and cinnamon somehow. She gripped his arms, and the response in his groin was damned near primal. He groaned against her mouth as her tongue flicked out to greet his.

She was never passive, and he loved that about her. His heart slammed in his chest as she laced her hand around his neck and pulled him more tightly to her.

He tore his mouth from her, knowing another minute of this and clothes would start to come off. He pressed his forehead to hers trying to give himself a moment to catch his breath.

"I don't think we're practicing anymore," he said.

She moved her head back and forth. "No. This doesn't feel like practice, does it?"

"Are you scared?" he asked.

"Terrified."

He put one hand behind her neck and pulled it in, eyes locked onto hers. "Don't be. I've got you."

Thoughts of guilt were swept away as they moved into her apartment and he stripped her down. She was incredible. He couldn't get enough of her as he worshipped with hands and mouth and tongue. As he whispered to her to let her know what she did to him. They moved together down the hall, his clothes coming off during the trip.

She writhed beneath him, responding to the smallest of touches, pleading with him for more. Her eyes darkened, a storm of passion and heat, urging him on. Her body spoke to him in a thousand ways, and he wanted to answer each and every one of them. He wanted to give her everything she needed and so much more. He was losing himself in her, but there was finding happening also. He was finding a new version of himself within her.

"Sara," he whispered when he entered her, and she reached for him, pressing up to meet him, as she pulled him down to kiss her. He kissed her fully, deeply, feeling her clamp down around his cock as she came with a keening moan. He followed swiftly after her, feeling the release with every ounce of his being. It was a release in every sense of the word.

CHAPTER 24

WARRICK RETURNED from the bathroom where he'd taken care of the condom to find Sara sitting up in her bed, an oversized T-shirt covering her body. He could see from the look on her face, he wasn't going to like where the conversation was headed. She chewed her bottom lip as she looked at him.

Okay. He grabbed his pants and pulled them on, then sat next to her on the bed. "Want to tell me what's going on?"

"Is it okay if I'm not ready for an overnight?" She looked at his chest as she asked, but he tilted her face up to meet his.

"I'm not going to push you for anything you're not ready for, Sara," he said. He had a feeling sleeping overnight in the same bed might be too much emotional connection for her. That it might be putting a little too much on the line.

In all fairness, he knew in his heart if he spent the night here, he'd hold her and love her through the night. With his body, that is.

But there would still be part of him he just didn't have

to give her. It wouldn't be fair. He shoved the thought aside
and kissed her, not wanting to face his own shortcomings.

"It's no problem, Sara. We'll move at whatever pace you
need to." *And we'll stop all this before we get too close.*

* * *

Sara controlled the shaking until she walked Warrick to the
door and kissed him goodnight. Then she went to the
bedroom and stood, staring, at the bed. That's when she let
herself fall apart. Her hand trembled as she removed her
prosthesis and stared down at the ugly stump at the end of
her wrist. It was sore and a little swollen.

He'd made her forget. In the restaurant, and even once
they'd come back here. That in itself was incredible. She
never thought she'd be with a man again.

But, the truth was, she wasn't ready to let him in
completely. Doing that would mean so much more. Letting
him between her legs was one thing. But there was no way
she could let him into her heart.

If she let him in, he'd eventually need to see her. All of
her. After all, she couldn't live in her prosthesis twenty-
four-seven. The skin would break down and she'd end up
with open sores in a matter of days.

If he spent any amount of time at her place, he'd see
that she needed a lot more modifications to her world than
the robotic hand he saw her in each day. When she was
home, she often had to go without her prosthesis, to let her
arm have a break from the strain of having the machinery
on. So, she required other tools in many parts of her world.

She had a special fork that had a cutting edge on one
side so she could cut her food one-handed. There was a
cutting board with prongs that held onto a piece of bread or

a vegetable so she could cut it. She had a clamp that held her toothbrush in place so she could put toothpaste on and another one to hold her hair dryer in place while she brushed her hair.

He would catch on very quickly that she dealt with phantom pain more than anyone realized. She used mirror therapy to address a lot of it, but by the end of the day she'd feel sharp pains going up fingertips that weren't there.

That had begun shortly after they'd made love. He'd left the bed, and almost immediately, at a time when most people would be relaxed and weak from pleasure, she'd been edgy and tense, knowing she needed to address the pain before it got any worse.

She sat at her vanity and pulled out the mirror she used for her therapy. She set it on the table, leaning it against her chest with an arm on either side of it. She focused on the mirror as her right hand went through stretching exercises and practiced movements. As she did it, her brain perceived her left hand making the same movements. It tricked the brain, somehow, and the pain began to ease.

She had a feeling, though, that she would still need to take a sleeping pill to sleep. On nights like this, the tension in her body never seemed to subside, even when the pain went away. She'd let herself get too tired, and for her, over-tired led to worse sleep.

Sara felt a large tear fall and watched where it landed on the desk as she leaned over it, working her arm. It pissed her off even more. She hated feeling sorry for herself. It wasn't who she was. But there were times she was almost too tired to fight it and she gave in and let herself throw a pity party. Now seemed like a good time. The first time she'd been with a man in years and she was going to need to knock herself out with a pill instead of falling asleep in his arms.

She bit down on the inside of her cheek and twisted her wrists, moving the muscles of both her complete arm and her stump in tandem, feeling the fingers of both hands stretch as she flexed and wiggled them. For just a moment, in Warrick's arms, she'd felt whole again.

It was incredible the tricks the mind could play.

CHAPTER 25

WARRICK TOSSED his keys on the side table in his entranceway and kicked off his shoes. He wouldn't let the fact that Sara hadn't wanted him to spend the night get to him. Hell, who would think the guy would be the one to get kicked out? The thought of it kind of made him laugh. It was supposed to be the man trying to run from the woman's bed, wasn't it?

He had no problem respecting her wishes. He would never force her into something she wasn't completely comfortable with. That didn't mean his mind didn't keep flashing back to the way their bodies felt tangled together, slick skin against slick skin. Being with Sara had been a hell of a lot more than he thought it would be. A hell of a lot more than he deserved.

He ignored the uncomfortable thought that he couldn't be what she deserved. That he couldn't give her any more than this. Not that he fully understood what *this* was. What he did know, though, was that things couldn't go past this. Not with his track record of letting people down. He couldn't give her more than friendship and sex.

Damned good sex, as it turned out. Even now, he wanted her again.

There was only one thing he could give her, and he would do all he could to make sure it happened. He could give her back her confidence. He could show her that only an asshole like her ex-fiancé would care whether she had one of her hands or not. He still couldn't believe the guy had walked out on her while she was still in the hospital.

She would never say it, but that had been a blow to her confidence. He would give her that back, and when it was time, he would leave her alone. He would let her move on to find somebody who could build a life with her. If anyone deserved it, Sara did. She deserved to have a family and a future with someone capable of giving love. Capable of receiving love.

Warrick began to head to the bedroom but turned instead toward the patio. He frowned when he saw the rose bush.

Shit. The leaves no longer had just a slightly yellowy tinge. Several had turned full-on yellow and the stalks of a few of the branches had turned black, almost like they were rotting from the inside out.

The sorrow that coursed through him seemed almost silly in a way. But that didn't make it hurt any less. He felt the familiar ache that came with letting someone down again. He backed up until his legs hit the couch, and sat, staring at the small plant. At least this time, he thought he'd done everything right. Everything he could for it. It didn't change things, though, did it?

As he sat and stared at the dying shrub, it was his wife he saw instead. His wife and the small baby who died with her. The baby he hadn't even known about until the doctors had told him in the hospital when his wife died.

That was the first time he drank himself into a stupor. And when he'd come out of it, he'd gone and got the rose-bush and planted it for his baby. Their baby. He had planted it right next to all the roses Vicki had planted and loved so much. And now he'd killed that too. Stupid as it was, he couldn't help but feel he'd let them down again.

Rage poured through him. Rage at himself for never getting it right.

Warrick's hand wrapped around the lamp next to him. He tightened his fingers around it, gripping so tightly his hand began to hurt. With a roar, he threw it across the room, hitting the wall where it shattered into pieces. A shattered life. How do you put that back together?

It wasn't enough. He stood and grabbed a fireplace poker, smashing the other lamps in the room, bathing it in darkness. It still wasn't enough, but the darkness suited his mood much better.

He crossed to the bar and reached for the bottle of Glenlivet, not bothering with the glass.

CHAPTER 26

DETECTIVE HARMON FELT the rush that came with the first big break in a case. This one had been too long in coming. They had gone back to see Meredith and Edward Ball, this time tackling the couple separately. Meredith Ball had talked.

Tyvek was more manipulative than Jarrod had given him credit for. He'd played the couple against each other. When Tyvek escaped the fire, he called Edward and convinced him Meredith had been in on his plan the entire time. That she'd been so set on expanding Branson Medical into the pharmaceutical industry, that she'd partnered with Tyvek on the promise that she'd get to develop the heart drug if the drug trials produced anything useful.

None of it had been true, but Edward Ball hadn't known that and he'd been willing to do anything to save his wife. By the time Meredith found out what was going on, Edward had been hiding Tyvek for weeks. The couple felt they didn't have any choice but to keep hiding him.

Jarrod watched as SWAT breached the apartment they

had leased in a fake name for Tyvek. It was a rundown kind of place. The type of place you could pay cash for and no one would ask any questions. That was exactly what they had done, which was why a run of their finances hadn't shown the small monthly payment being made. They had simply taken it out of the pocket money they already withdrew from the bank each month.

Jarrod listened to the calls of "clear" coming from the officers in the apartment, cursing under his breath because he knew that meant Tyvek was no longer here. He and Cal entered as the team lead came back to the living room.

"No sign of him, but he's been here recently. There's a wet toothbrush in the bathroom and food scraps in the sink that are day-old at best," the man said as his team filed out into the hallway.

Jarrod nodded. "You guys clear out as fast as you can. Hopefully he hasn't seen us. We'll take a look around here, then post a couple of undercover guys to wait for him to come back."

The SWAT team left almost as quickly as they had come and Cal and Jarrod did a quick search of the apartment. It was small, with peeling paint and only a kitchenette, living space with bed, and bathroom.

"You see anything useful?" Cal asked a minute later, coming out of the bathroom.

"Nothing that tells us where he is. I called into the station and the captain has two undercover guys on their way. They'll text when they're in place, but we need to get out of here. How about you?"

Cal held up the packaging from a box of hair dye. "I'm guessing Tyvek is now a brunette."

"Can that stuff really cover a guy as gray as Tyvek was?"

William Tyvek had had a full head of gray hair, not just a little salt and pepper throughout. He'd always seemed like one of the most recognizable guys to Jarrod, but maybe if you took him out of the designer suits and got rid of his fancy haircut and manicures, the guy could pass for average.

"Apparently." Cal turned over the box to show an image of a man with a full head of gray hair next to an image of the same man, now brown-haired and looking easily ten years younger.

"Shit. That's a pretty major difference." The image was striking and Jarrod struggled to imagine what the change would do to Tyvek. Maybe one of the forensic artists could help them figure out what he'd look like now.

"Still, Tyvek is a pretty well-known face around the city. He's got to be doing something else to cover his looks."

"I don't know. How much of his look had to do with the suits and the fancy cars and things? Would he be as memorable in jeans and a hoodie without a chauffeur?"

Cal's only response was a curse.

"We need to see if Meredith or Edward Ball has seen him. We need to know what he looks like."

Cal agreed. "I'll reach out to them. Can you get with the captain and make sure the undercovers headed this way know what to look for?"

"You think it's worth the risk to canvas the neighbors right now?"

"No. Let's give him a day to come back, then we'll canvas."

* * *

Tyvek continued walking straight instead of turning at the corner. He couldn't take a chance that the SWAT vehicle was at the apartment building for him. It had been a miracle they hadn't found him before this. He didn't have much time left. It was time to finish what he'd started.

CHAPTER 27

IT TOOK Warrick a minute to figure out why his head was pounding and his mouth felt like someone had planted wheat stalks in there overnight. He had broken a rule he never broke. When the grief had swamped him after Vicki and his baby died, he'd been so damned tempted to bury himself in a bottle. But he'd also been smart. He knew damned well if he went down that road he wouldn't come back out of there.

So he limited himself carefully, always maintaining complete control. Except for the one night of the year when he let himself go. Now, he'd broken the rule, getting completely sloshed in an effort to erase the guilt, the memories, the feelings. He thought he could do this with Sara. That he could let some feeling back in and maintain control.

He was wrong. There couldn't be any halfway on this. Letting himself feel meant he had to feel it all, face it all. As it turned out, he wasn't as strong as he thought he was. Not nearly as in control as he'd hoped to be.

He eyed the empty bottle next to the couch and the

mass of broken glass in the corner of the room. He stood and walked to the patio. Apparently, he'd gone after the rose shrub at some point the night before. There was now a broken branch and a crack down the center of the largest stem. If it wasn't dead before, it was dead now. He stared at it blankly before pulling out his phone.

Plenty of missed texts and calls.

"Charlotte," he said when his assistant answered the phone, "I need you to cover things for me for a little bit at the office." He looked at the clock on the microwave. It was 9 a.m. She'd already been covering for him for an hour at work since he'd had meetings scheduled at eight. But that wasn't what he meant.

"For the morning?" She asked, her voice holding a tone of uncertainty.

"No," he said rubbing his temple. "I'll be gone through Friday, maybe longer." He could hear the stunned silence at the other end of the line. "Cancel what you can, handle anything that can be handled, just put people off."

"Is everything all right?" He knew she had to be worried to ask that kind of question. Charlotte was old school. She was the type who believed in privacy.

"Everything is fine. I just... Need to go away." He didn't know where he was going. Maybe he'd start house hunting for that cabin in the woods.

He still had a place in the woods, but William Tyvek had used that cabin to kill one of the scientists working with him. He'd left the body there to make it look like Warrick was the killer. Charlotte had arranged for some crime scene cleaning company to clean it out, but somehow, the idea of going there didn't appeal. They'd listed it for sale, but word was out about the dead body. Funny how that slowed things down.

He could go look for something else now, though. Maybe he could figure out his next step. Things at Simms were getting back on track. The cousins didn't seem to be calling for his retirement any longer. Sales had been coming back into line with what they'd seen before all this started. It was time for him to start thinking about where to go from here.

"Oh and Charlotte?"

"Yes?"

"Can you have somebody come and clean my condo while I'm gone?" He had a regular cleaning service that came every week, but he didn't want to leave all this broken glass for them to find. "It's, uh, it's a bit of a mess."

"Of course. I'll send someone over. Is tomorrow okay for that?" He knew she was asking if he'd be there when they came or if she could send them anytime.

"That's fine. I'll be gone by then." He hung up the phone and went to pack a bag.

CHAPTER 28

SARA LOOKED AT THE CLOCK. It was noon but she had accomplished next to nothing all morning. She hated to admit it, but she'd been looking at the door to her office all morning. She kept thinking Warrick would come through it at any minute.

Part of her, a big part of her, wanted to see him. Another part of her didn't know what to say if he did come. It was why she hadn't gone to see him herself. She was chickening out.

Would he be upset that she'd sent him away the night before? Would things be awkward? Or would he tell her he regretted what had happened? That they needed to go back to just being friends with an occasional kiss? Or friends without the kissing?

Not friends at all? Clearly, sitting and stewing on the matter wasn't helping her.

She didn't know what to think about the fact that he hadn't come to see her at all. Then again, it was entirely possible he was waiting for her to come to him. After all, she was the one who had set the boundary last night. So maybe he was letting her make the next move.

She looked at her desk, searching for some excuse to go up and see him. She didn't find any answers on her desk, but she stood anyway. She could come up with something on the way up in the elevator. She could always ask him if he wanted her to contact Jax Cutter about developing a prosthesis for lower limb loss.

Or maybe she'd grow a spine on the way up and just say she had come to see him. To ask what next. Nothing like the direct route.

She exited the elevator on the top floor and made her way down the hall toward Warrick's office. Charlotte sat at her desk outside, as expected. But the double doors of his office stood open. She could see before she even approached Charlotte, that the room is empty. She pasted a smile on her face.

"Is he in?" For the most part, nowadays, if Warrick wasn't on a conference call or in a meeting, Charlotte would waive Sara past her.

Instead, today she frowned. "No, I'm afraid not. He's out for the rest of the week."

Disappointment slammed into Sara. Disappointment and humiliation. Because if he left for the week and hadn't told her, last night hadn't meant anything to him. Right? She hadn't been this confused in a long time.

She nodded, unable to speak past the lump in her throat. She should have known. It was stupid really, for her to read more into it. They said right from the start they would be friends that would kiss occasionally. So what if kissing had moved into sex? That didn't mean that the sex meant any more than the kisses had.

"Do you want me to try to reach him for you?" Charlotte asked, a hint of something in her voice that Sara couldn't place. Pity?

Wonderful. Now she'd gone from self-pity to pity from others. Was that a move up or a move down? She really didn't know. But she didn't like it. She remembered that saying about changing your reaction to something when you couldn't change the thing itself. That's what she needed to do. She couldn't control what had happened with Warrick. She couldn't go back and make changes but she could change her response.

"No," she said shaking her head, trying for an air of indifference. "I just had a question for him, but it can wait."

She turned before Charlotte could see through her bull-shit, but she had a feeling the woman wasn't fooled. Charlotte had the ability to see through any smoke screen.

Sara walked stiffly back to the elevator and got herself to her office before she let the tears fall. She honestly felt like she was crying over so many things at once, and maybe it was time she'd let herself mourn a few things.

This wasn't just about Warrick. She was crying because Mitchell had walked out on her all those years ago, opening a wound in her that would probably never heal. She was crying because last night she had let herself believe, even for the smallest of moments, that maybe she could have a normal relationship. She was crying because she knew deep down she had fallen for Warrick Staunton. She had fallen for him in a big way, and now it looked like her heart would be stomped on once again.

CHAPTER 29

TWO DAYS in a cabin had turned out to be enough for Warrick. So much for his new life plan. It had been more than just the emptiness of not having anything to do. He could have handled that. This cabin had been more rustic than the one his family owned. He hadn't wanted to go there. Not only had Tyvek killed a man there, it brought back memories of Vicki and him. Not to mention, it didn't really qualify as a cabin. It was more like a luxury home except for being made from logs rather than drywall or brick.

The cabin he'd rented had a lake right outside the door and hiking trails through the woods. It had a wood burning stove and small kitchenette. It met the definition of cabin in more than a cursory sense. And that meant there was little to do there and it was awfully quiet. The biggest problem with it, though, had been that Sara wasn't there with him.

He had wanted Sara. He wanted to hold her and make love to her. But he also wanted to talk to her, to hear her laugh, to have her take away that heavy weight that sat in his gut all day every day.

She would have made hiking through the woods fun. She'd likely have found a way to engineer fishing poles out of scotch tape and a paper clip so they could make use of the lake. That was the kind of thing she did. She could make something out of nothing. She could make him feel human again.

On the third night, Warrick got in his car and made the four-and-a-half-hour trip home. It was almost midnight when he got in.

He opened his condo door to find his Uncle Jonathan pawing through his mail. "Jonathan? Jesus, what are you doing here?" His thoughts went to his mother. Maybe something was wrong with her. Or Sara. *Hell.* "Is everything okay?"

Jonathan spun, anger in his eyes. "No, everything is not okay. You took off. You didn't tell Charlotte where you were going. You didn't call me or your mother. And you think everything is okay?" As he spoke Jonathan crossed the room, closing the distance between him and Warrick.

Warrick half expected him to strike him, but Jonathan pulled him in and hugged him tight to his chest. Warrick stood frozen, then brought his arms up, half surprising himself when he returned the hug.

His uncle held on for a long minute then stepped back and looked at Jonathan. "Where were you? I've been going through your place trying to figure out where you might've gone. I know you sold the beach house and you sold that monstrosity you bought for Vicki. I had the sheriff drive out to the cabin even though we've had that closed tight since the murder, but you weren't there. I've been out of my mind. I couldn't figure out where else you would've gone. I called the caretakers at your mother's place thinking you might be in the guesthouse but they hadn't seen you on the grounds anywhere."

Jonathan sank into the couch and Warrick sat next to him, surprised to see his uncle was shaking a bit. "I'm so sorry. I didn't think—" He was so used to his uncle being a bit scatterbrained and not checking in for days, it hadn't even occurred to him that his uncle would worry about him. "I went up to New Hampshire, rented a place. I thought maybe I'd get away for a little while but it turns out I suck at getting away."

"And all this?" Jonathan waved his arm toward the empty end tables and the patio that still held the empty planter where the rosebush had stood. The dead shrub was gone and the glass and ceramic had been swept away. "You want to tell me what spurred this little getaway of yours?"

Warrick lowered his face to his hands and scrubbed it. "Things were just getting a little too, uh, stressful here."

"You mean you were getting too close to Sara here?"

Warrick's eyebrows shot up. He didn't know his uncle could be that intuitive. The man was a scientist through and through. Intuition never seemed to play a big part in his makeup. "Yeah, that."

"Have you told her any of it?"

"Any of what?"

"Any of why you and Vicki fell apart?"

"No. I'm not sure I can answer that question for myself much less for somebody else. Besides, Sara has her own issues to work through. She doesn't need to deal with my shit."

The lines in Jonathan's face deepened. "Did you tell her about the baby?"

Just hearing the word "baby" felt like a knife twisting

into Warrick's gut. He was stunned that it had come from his uncle. "You know about the baby?"

Jonathan nodded. "You talk about it sometimes on your binge nights." His uncle had always seemed to be around when Warrick needed someone to get him into bed at the end of his anniversary nights. That's what they call them, the anniversary nights. The anniversary of the night he let his family down. He had to wonder how much more Jonathan knew if he'd been talking when he was drunk. Did he know Warrick had let Vicki walk out even though he knew she was too high and wasted to drive?

"Have you talked to Sara about it?" Jonathan tried again.

Warrick shook his head. "No. She knows a little bit about Vicki, but she doesn't know everything."

"You know I've been waiting for you to get over this by yourself. I kept telling myself Warrick is a strong guy, a smart man. But here you are, three years later and still feeling sorry for yourself."

Warrick laughed, letting the bitterness rising like bile in his throat mingle with the laughter and come out in its tone. "I'm not feeling sorry for myself. I'm watching out for Sara. How can I let somebody else in my life after I let down everyone around me? After what I did to Vicki? To our baby?"

"What is it that you think you've done?"

Now Warrick started to raise his voice, something he had never done with his uncle. With his dad? Oh yeah. There's been a lot of screaming between the two of them. But his uncle had always listened to him. Had always had time for him.

"Don't you get it? Vicki would never have gone back to drugs and drinking if it weren't for me. She was clean. She was off that shit. And you know what she wanted? All she ever wanted? Was to be a mom. She wanted a family. Not only did I not give her that, when she asked if we could adopt, do you know what I said?" He didn't wait for an answer. "I said no. What the hell kind of a husband says no when his wife asks if they can adopt a baby? I told her if the baby wasn't my own I didn't want it."

"That was your father speaking, not you, Warrick." Jonathan's voice was quiet, but there was a firmness to it that wasn't always present. "If you told her that, it was because your father had convinced you that you needed to give him an heir."

Another burst of that bitter laugh. "On his deathbed. He told me on his deathbed that even my sperm couldn't live up to his standards."

Jonathan's sigh was heavy. "Warrick, your father was a cruel man and an ass. He was one of those people who was never happy with himself, so he had to make sure the people around him felt as bad or worse than he did."

Warrick didn't answer. Jonathan wasn't telling him anything he didn't already know. Jonathan continued anyway. "But what you don't realize is that you're the polar opposite. You're not happy with yourself, so you think you don't deserve anything good in this world. That you deserve to pay the price forever for some imagined failings. And they *are* imagined," he said when Warrick opened his mouth to argue. "Vicki was an adult. She made the choice to use drugs again, to get in that car when she had no business driving. I know you loved her from the time you guys were just kids, but that's all the more reason for you to know that her problems started long before you could take the blame for any of them. She was sick when she was younger and her dad didn't do right by her. He didn't get her the kind of help she needed. You know that. In your heart, you know it. You just need to find a way to get your head to believe that. To let yourself forgive."

He stood, leaving Warrick to think about what he'd said. His uncle stopped when he got to the door. "Sara is a pretty incredible woman. You deserve to have someone like her in your life, and I know you don't believe you're good enough for her, but that's just bumpkis, Warrick. Plain and simple."

Warrick shook his head. "Bumpkis, huh?"

"It's a technical term," Jonathan said. "Look it up," He turned and let himself out while Warrick shook his head.

CHAPTER 30

"YOU HAVEN'T HEARD from him at all?" Samantha asked. She and Sara sat in Samantha's living room. Samantha's husband, Logan, had taken over baby duties and put baby Joey down to bed, then left Samantha and Sara to talk.

Sara shook her head no, then took a sip of her wine.

He'd made her feel so good, so wanted. So much like the woman she used to be. She wanted that to last. She wanted it back.

"Oh honey, I'm so sorry."

Sara tried to smile, but it was weak. She wouldn't let herself cry any more, but she was having a little trouble with the smiling thing. Samantha moved closer to her on the couch and pulled her in for a hug. Sara accepted the hug for a good long while. When they pulled apart, Samantha put her wine glass back in her hands, then refilled it from the bottle.

"He'll come around, hon. He's probably just scared or in a panic. From what I've heard, he mourned for his wife for a long time."

"I don't think he's ever stopped." Sara knew he hadn't.

He didn't talk about Vicki all the time or anything like that. He was too careful to do that. Too in control. But she knew he wasn't over her. It was in everything he did. She could see the sorrow and the self-blame written on his face at times.

"Oh, honey." Samantha rubbed Sara's arm.

Sara laughed a little. "You've said that a few times."

Samantha laughed, too. "Sorry. I just wish I knew what to say. I can call him a pig and an ass if you want. That's helpful, right? He's a total ass!"

"Ha! Yes, that helps." Her face crumpled again. "Except he's not. He's really not. I mean, I get it. He loved his wife. I know there's more going on there that he hasn't told me, but I think he feels guilty for her death. Like he should have been able to stop it. I think he blames himself for her addiction." She'd always known there was more going on with Vicki's death than he'd shared with her. Maybe with anyone. It wasn't like the man was an open book. There was a part of him that was unreachable.

She guessed he would say the same about her, though. The irony wasn't lost on her.

"Oh that poor man," Samantha said, making Sara laugh again. Samantha couldn't help it. She really did feel for everyone. It was what made her such a good friend.

Sara smirked. "You're supposed to be feeling for me not him."

Samantha raised her hands up. "What can I say? It's like you're two people who both totally deserve love and a happily ever after, but you're both sort of floating and lost because you've been hurt so badly in the past."

Sara pulled her knees up, resting her chin on them. "Yeah, love sucks."

"Love?"

She sighed. "You know what I mean. Potential love is the right way to say it, I guess." As she spoke, she brushed aside the feeling that this had somehow gone past potential for her. She didn't how it happened and she didn't know what to do about it, but she felt very much like she was lying to herself and to her friend. Potential love was a load of horse crap and she knew it.

CHAPTER 31

WARRICK PACED his living room floor. He'd showered and tried to sleep, but that had lasted all of five minutes. There was no denying it—he wanted Sara. He wanted to be with her, and not just tonight. He wanted more with her.

He just had to find out if she could accept him as he was. Could she handle it if he was honest? If he explained he could love her, be with her, but had to hold back a piece of his heart from her. That he couldn't love her with all of himself, all his heart. That he had to protect himself on some level.

She would understand that. In fact, he reasoned, she might want the same thing herself. To build a life together, but not be wholly vulnerable to the kind of pain they'd both been through in the past. She'd been hurt, too, and he recognized she avoided commitment, avoided putting herself out there because of it. They could make this work.

He eyed the clock then paced the length of the floor again. It was after midnight. Could he really show up at her door? *Screw it.*

He threw on a pair of sneakers and grabbed his car keys.

Warrick left through the back door of the building, cutting directly across the lot to his car. He would lay it out for Sara. She would understand.

Ten minutes later, he took her front steps two at a time, relieved to see the lights on in the living room. He knocked softly.

She took his breath away when she answered. She looked freshly showered and she wore a long sweatshirt and socks. The sweatshirt came to her thighs and if he had to guess, she wasn't wearing anything under it. That wasn't what took his breath. It was the kick to the gut when he saw that she'd been crying.

She didn't say anything, but she lifted her chin a little as if to dare him to screw with her.

"Sara," he breathed and reached for her. He pulled her to him and she came, for a moment. Her body melted against his and her arms came around his back. But then she pushed out of his hold.

"You left." There was accusation and sadness in her voice.

"I'm sorry. I'd like to explain. If I can."

She stepped back and let him in, and he took her hand and drew her to the couch, pulling her down next to him. She seemed to fit so perfectly, leaning against him like she was made to fit as she curled into him and he wrapped his arms around her.

"I missed you."

"Where did you go?" She asked the question without judgment now as if she was willing to listen.

"To New Hampshire."

"Trying out cabin life?"

He grinned and nodded. "It didn't work out."

"Tell me about it." She took one of his hands in hers and he began to tell her about Vicki.

He told Sara about Vicki's need to fill some emptiness inside of her that he could never understand. His failure to be there for her, to understand she needed more from him. "By the time I had decided it was silly not to adopt a child, she'd gone back to drinking and using drugs. I couldn't bring a baby into that."

He took a slow breath. "It took me so long to figure out that it didn't matter if a baby was ours or not. We would have loved any child. It just took me too damned long."

His voice sounded hollow when he spoke the next words. "I let her leave that night. There'd been so many nights of fighting. So many times I tried to get through to her. But I knew that night she'd been drinking. I was just so tired of trying to stop her. I let her down. I let our baby down."

Sara turned to look at him and there was so much sorrow in her eyes. "Oh no. No, Warrick."

He nodded.

She cupped his face with her hand. "I'm so sorry." She was quiet a minute. "So you and Vicki didn't know?"

"I honestly don't know if she did. I've come to believe she couldn't have. She wanted to be a mother so badly. I don't think she would have done anything to harm our baby if she knew." He shook his head. "I don't know, though. The addiction seemed to have hold of her so tightly that last time. I just don't know."

Sara didn't tell him it wasn't his fault. Didn't say he should have stopped her from getting in the car. Didn't absolve him. And for that, he was glad. He didn't want that.

He'd started to come to terms with the way he let Vicki down. But he didn't want forgiveness for it. That wasn't something he deserved. He didn't know if Sara somehow knew it would be empty words for him. He wasn't ready to hear it yet. He probably wouldn't ever get there.

"I really want to be with you. You make me feel things I haven't felt in so long, Sara. You make me feel almost whole again." He could see the wariness in her eyes. "I just can't let myself love again. I can't do that—can't go through it again. It gutted me when I lost Vicki and the baby. I can't be in that position again."

She laid her head on his shoulder and he watched as her chest rose and fell softly. She was still for a few minutes before she laughed.

He found himself smiling. "You're laughing?"

"I'm sorry," she waived her hand. "It's not funny. It's just, I'm not ready to really let someone in either. I think I made that clear when I sort of freaked the other night and made you leave."

"Ah, that. Yeah, that was something. You wanna tell me about that?"

She fidgeted, but answered. "I just guess I'm not ready to have anyone really close again."

"Because they might leave if it gets too heavy?"

"Yeah. Something like that."

"We're a pair." He brought her hand up and kissed the soft skin on the inside of her wrist.

She made a soft sound and he knew he didn't want this to end. He had no idea where they were going and he knew they were both broken. That had to make this a bad idea. But he wasn't ready to walk away.

"Do you want to try? Try being a couple, Sara?"

"It sounds like a horrible idea," she looked up at him

and leaned into him a bit, and he pulled her to straddle his lap, settling her in and lining them up just where he needed her to be.

He ran his hands up her back, pressing as he went until she slid closer. "Can you live with that?" He brushed his lips against hers as she wriggled closer still.

She nodded. "Can you live with going home at the end of the night? Until I'm ready for more than that?"

He had to admit, he wanted to say no. He wanted to make love then wrap her in his arms and hold her. He didn't want to go home and spend the night alone. But he would take what she'd give him for now. "Yes. I can live with that."

She leaned her head to the side as he trailed kisses down her neck, loving the sounds that came from her in response. She ground down into him. He'd been hard already, but now he needed to be inside of her. Needed to bury himself deep within her as she wrapped herself around him.

He pulled the sweatshirt she wore up over her head and she brought her arms up, letting him slip it off. The pair of lace panties he revealed did little to cover her from him and he groaned at the sight of her.

"You're incredible." He dropped the sweatshirt and ran his hands down her torso and over her thighs. Her skin was silky soft and the slightest touch of his hands to it made his erection scream for more. He wanted to lick and bite and tease every damned inch of her. He wanted her moaning his name and wrapping her legs around him as she came. He wanted to feel her as she came on his cock, milking him again and again.

* * *

Sara was lost in the sensation of Warrick's hands and mouth

on her. He had the ability to take her out of reality so easily, it sometimes shocked her. He could make her forget things and just *feel*.

Need and want spiraled in her. He closed his mouth around one nipple and the wet heat sent another flood of arousal through her. When he moved to the other breast, she let out a low moan and pulled at his shirt. She wanted to see him, touch him. She needed more from him. So much more.

He pulled his shirt over his head. She ran her right hand over his shoulder and chest, reveling in the heat, feeling the taught muscles underneath the skin. There was just enough hair on his chest to tickle and tease her hand. She moved her hand up to his head as his tongue did things to her nipples that had her body pulsing with need. He raised his face to hers and the look in his eyes told her he felt the same way she did.

She licked her lips and dropped her eyes, taking in the sight of him before her. She'd thought this would never happen again. That they'd never be together again like this.

He put his hand around the back of her head and pulled gently on her hair, directing her eyes to his. "Someday, I'm going to get you to forget all of it. Not to worry about what I think or if I might run."

He sealed that promise with a kiss before standing and letting her slide down his body. Within minutes, he had his pants and boxers off and her panties somehow disappeared. Then he was kneeling in front of her doing things to her that made her grip his hair in her hands begging him not to stop.

He didn't stop. Not until she came apart in his arms and he had to hold her up as her body went week from her orgasm.

When he took her to the bedroom and entered her, she felt full and whole and complete. He kissed her with long drugging kisses as he moved in her, deep and hard. Every part of her body responded, panting with the need to come again.

Her body felt so right in his arms, as though she belonged with him. As though he belonged with her. It was more than a physical sensation, and on some level, it scared her.

He whispered to her as they made love. Words like incredible and beautiful. Words that made her believe he might never walk away from her. She shoved aside that belief. She couldn't handle the weight of it, the risk. Couldn't let herself put faith in it.

She moved her body with each thrust of his hips, twisting as he entered her again and again. Each plunge sent that sweet feeling within her spiraling higher and higher and she knew he was getting closer to coming. She could feel it, see it as their bodies moved together. She didn't want this to end.

Warrick bent close to her ear, letting his teeth graze the lobe as he nipped at her. If she'd thought her body couldn't take any more, she was wrong. He shifted and pressed deeper still, lifting her hips in his large hands as his penis pressed a spot that made her pant with need and claw at his back. It was too much and not enough all at once.

"Let me see you come again, Sara," he whispered, then drew back to watch her face. She felt exposed, but somehow, she trusted him to see her in such a vulnerable way. Trusted that she could let herself go. That with Warrick, there didn't have to be any holding back. "Show me, Sara."

Her orgasm built slowly but when it hit her, she cried out as waves of sweet pleasure poured over her. She heard

Warrick's growl as he came with her and knew, she'd given a small piece of her heart to him. She hadn't meant to. She'd meant to keep it locked down tight, but he'd somehow edged his way in and chipped away at her defenses. And she didn't know how to stop him.

CHAPTER 32

A WEEK of seeing Sara every night made it that much more difficult not to see her. So, when Warrick flew back home after a meeting in New York, he wasn't eager to head to bed without seeing her. Never mind that it was past midnight.

He tried to stay away. He even changed into shorts and a tee-shirt, planning to watch TV in bed until he was tired enough to fall asleep. He stared at the bed and argued with himself.

She'd be awake. He'd come to realize she was a night owl. Some nights, she'd let him hang out for a while after they made love, and he'd watch her work on prototypes for different prostheses or mess around taking something apart to see how it worked. Her mind fascinated him. It seemed to work in ways that his mind couldn't even grasp and she was beautiful when she got so deep in thought about something she forgot he was there.

It was times like those he realized she was in more pain than she'd let on. She'd forget he was watching and start to rub her arm. Then she'd realize what she was doing and he'd be sent packing soon after. He had a feeling she wasn't ready for him to see that she required any kind of self-care. Like somehow admitting she needed anything might be admitting a weakness.

If he was honest with himself, his walls weren't doing a very good job of protecting his heart. She was getting under his skin and into his heart and soul in a way he wasn't ready to face. Ignoring what was happening worked better for him for the time being.

Screw it. He grabbed his phone, wallet, and car keys. He'd be useless in the office tomorrow if he spent the next few hours with Sara before driving home to catch a few hours of sleep, but he didn't care. He needed her.

The thought slammed home and his chest tightened. He did need her. His footsteps slowed as he crossed the parking lot and realized, he'd come to need her a lot more than he'd admitted. He wanted more.

He stared at his car door handle and asked himself if he could let himself love her. Could he go to that place again where he was vulnerable to the kind of pain Vicki's death had brought him? Could he trust that he wouldn't let Sara down the way he'd let down Vicki and the baby?

There wasn't any doubt in his mind. He was already there. It had snuck up on him and there was no turning back now. And he knew he was a different person than he'd been with Vicki. He and Vicki had loved each other from the time they were young. But somehow, what they had had been poisoned. He'd never been able to fill the hole inside her, and she'd never been able to believe she was enough. They'd just never been strong enough to overcome that.

He and Sara each had their issues, but he knew they could overcome that. They had to. Because he was in love with her already, and he'd bet she felt the same for him.

He wouldn't make the same mistakes this time. He wouldn't let his pride get in the way of what was best for him and Sara. Of what was best for their relationship and the family he hoped to build with her.

Now he had to hope he could convince her to let him in. To let her walls down and see that he wasn't going to leave her like her fiancé had. That he was in this forever. If she didn't believe him he'd just have to show her. He would prove it to her again and again. Eventually, she'd see it was true.

He grinned. No matter how long it took, he'd wait for her. He'd have patience enough for both of them. He reached for the car door and froze as a strange feeling stabbed at the back of his neck.

Then it hit him. The parking lot was dark. It hadn't been when he'd come in only half an hour before.

The scuffle of a shoe sounded on the blacktop behind him and he realized the lights in the parking lot were both out. No, not out. Smashed.

Shit. That was the last thought he had before he saw the movement out of the corner of his eye. By then, it was too late. There was nothing he could do to ward off the blow.

CHAPTER 33

WARRICK STRUGGLED to open his eyes as sharp pain ricocheted through his skull and a wave of nausea swamped him.

What the fuck?

He couldn't make any sense of anything, but he knew something was very, very wrong. His gut clenched as his thoughts flew to Sara, but he quickly remembered she wasn't with him. He'd been alone.

Alone when someone had hit him.

His hands were bound, not to mention numb. And he was in the back seat of a car. Time slowed while he fought the disorientation.

His car. He breathed slowly through his nose. His mouth was covered with duct tape. He tried to think through the fog that seemed to fill his head. The car wasn't moving and there wasn't anyone else in it. He lay on his side half on the seat and half slumped over the center console that divided the two seats in the back, as though someone had dumped him there.

The door opened and a man's face leaned in. He knew the face, but it took him a minute to place it. Something was off. The hair was different. Warrick almost laughed at how changing the simple color of the man's hair and the angry scar on his cheek had completely changed the man's appearance. It didn't seem possible.

Warrick stared into the face of his former father-in-law. William Tyvek wasn't on the run. He was right here.

Warrick began to curse the man through the tape over his mouth, anger coursing through his veins at all the man had done. It was then he noticed the look in the man's eye. It was the look of a true madman.

Tyvek looked over his shoulder, then back at Warrick, a look of amusement crossing his face, though Warrick couldn't begin to fathom what was so entertaining to the man. How could he take pleasure in all he'd done?

When he and Vicki had been growing up, Tyvek had been uncompromising and strict, but he had always loved his daughter. How does a man who loved someone the way Tyvek had loved Vicki turn into such a monster?

"Sorry, Warrick. I can't have you drawing attention to us. She'll be here soon." He raised a syringe and plunged it into Warrick's arm.

She? Vicki? Was Tyvek that far gone?

"She'll come, and then we'll get started."

Warrick's eyes flew to the building behind Tyvek. The Simms logo. They were in front of his office building. Why the hell would they be here?

As his brain grew fuzzy and a wave of heaviness washed over him from the drug, the answer came to Warrick. Tyvek wasn't talking about Vicki.

Sara. Tyvek was going after Sara.

Warrick fought to stay conscious. He needed to stop

this. To stop whatever Tyvek had in mind. He couldn't—
wouldn't—lose Sara. He couldn't see another woman he
loved destroyed.

CHAPTER 34

SARA HAD TAKEN the sidewalk surrounding the park instead of the path that cut through it. She'd bought an extra coffee in case she ran into one of the regulars who hung out in the park. As she rounded the corner, she saw Buddy shuffling toward her. He raised his head and caught sight of her, and his face transformed. She smiled and waved.

He'd started talking to her more and more, and it turned out, he was a really funny guy. She was pretty sure he made up most of what he told her, but she didn't care. It made her laugh and he seemed to have fun making her laugh. Who was she to object?

She was twenty feet from him when a car pulled up.

No, not *a* car. Warrick's car. But it wasn't Warrick behind the wheel.

Sara walked to the passenger side window and leaned over to look in. The man behind the wheel leaned toward her as the window came down.

And then her heart stopped. He held a gun. Only it wasn't pointed at her. If it had been pointed at her, she could have run. He was inside the car, making it hard for him to get a clear shot at her if she sprinted toward the back of the car instead of turning to run directly away.

He must have known she would try. He had his weapon pointed at a figure in the back. An unconscious and bound Warrick with dried blood on one side of his face.

Sara's heart slammed in her chest at the sight and she stepped closer. His breathing looked shallow. Too shallow.

She swallowed hard as her brain raced for some way out of this. It had to be a mistake, right? Maybe a dream. No, a nightmare.

But she was painfully aware that it was no dream. She couldn't be more awake.

"Get in the car, sweetheart," the man said. Sara's eyes flew to him. His tone was all wrong. He spoke to her as if he knew her, as if he were picking up a friend or family member. He'd called her sweetheart in a tender way. Who does that with a gun in their hand?

There was something familiar about him, and yet, she was almost positive she didn't know him. Did she?

Scenarios flew through Sara's mind, but there wasn't an end to this where she could run away and leave Warrick with this man. Sara glanced to where Buddy was still ambling toward her. His eyes caught hers and she could see the confusion on his face. Good. She could use that.

She dropped the coffees she held, letting them fall to her feet. She took one last hard look at Buddy, hoping he would realize something was wrong. *Please, let him realize there was something wrong.*

Then she turned away. She closed her eyes and took a deep breath, opened the car door and stepped in.

CHAPTER 35

JARROD HARMON TOOK one look at Darla and the man she was dragging behind her and knew something was wrong. Darla avoided the police station at all costs. It took a lot for her to come down here and seek him out.

He stood as she came through the doors to the major crimes unit. "Darla, what is it?"

She was breathing as though she'd run all the way to the precinct. "Sara is in trouble." She frowned a bit. "We think. Maybe."

"Sara?" Jarrod tried to think back through to the friends of Darla's that he'd met, but none were ringing a bell.

Darla nodded and pulled her friend forward. "Tell him, Buddy."

The man ducked his eyes and nodded but didn't say anything.

"Buddy saw Sara this morning. She was coming to bring him coffee like she always does, then someone picked her up in a car. But the thing is, she didn't bring Buddy his coffee. She dropped it on the ground and she looks at Buddy all funny like there's something wrong."

As tips went, it wasn't a great one, but something in Jarrod's gut tightened. "Do you mean Sara Blackburn? Warrick Staunton's girlfriend?"

"Yeah, Sara." Darla nodded at Jarrod like she was resisting calling him an idiot. Either that or simply thankful he was finally catching on.

"Buddy, what made you think something was wrong, other than the look she gave you?"

"I think there was a gun," Buddy said quietly. "The man had a gun on her."

He frowned and dialed Warrick's number. No answer.

He dialed the number for Simms Pharmaceutical next, raising his hand to wave his partner, Cal, over in the meantime. He spoke briefly with Warrick's assistant before hanging up. He quickly filled Cal in.

"Warrick and Sara are both no-shows at work. The assistant said she can't reach either of them. They aren't returning calls and Sara has missed a couple of meetings she'd scheduled this morning."

"You think this could be linked to Tyvek?"

Jarrod shrugged. "Could be nothing. It's hard to know at this point. Warrick's assistant is checking the parking lot for their cars. She'll call us back." He turned to Buddy. "Did you get a look at the man in the car?"

Buddy shook his head. "Not really," he mumbled. "Saw the gun, though. He held it up at her, then pointed it into the back seat."

"What kind of car was it? Do you know the make or the color? Any idea of the plate number?"

"Fancy. Real fancy. Black. License plate started with TZ3."

"Cal—"

"On it," Cal said, sitting in front of his computer screen

and slapping away at the keys before Jarrod even made the request. He paused a minute before looking up. "Warrick Staunton drives a black Mercedes Maybach. License plate matches."

Cal hit a few more keys, then turned the monitor toward Buddy. "Is this the car you saw?"

Buddy nodded. "That's it." For once, there seemed to be some power behind his words instead of the doubt they'd heard so far. "That's the one I saw."

Cal pulled up a picture of Warrick. "Was this the man driving?"

Buddy shook his head slowly and shrugged. Jarrod took it to mean the man didn't know. Call pulled up the photo they'd gotten from one of the computer guys. They'd taken an old image of William Tyvek and given him brown hair to see what he would look like if he was the one who'd used the hair dye at the apartment they had raided. Tyvek never showed back up to the place.

A canvas of the neighbors had been a little more helpful. The woman across the hall had been only too happy to help them. She was plump and happy, at least until they mentioned her neighbor. Then she'd scowled and said he was rude and didn't talk to anyone. Kathi Gilliam had told them the picture the computer guys had come up with wasn't too far off. She'd told them to lighten the hair a bit and add a scar to his right cheek.

Cal showed the picture to Buddy. "Could this be him?"

Another shrug.

Shit. They might or might not have a crime. Sara might or might not be in danger. Warrick Staunton or William Tyvek might or might not be involved. Perfect.

CHAPTER 36

SARA'S MIND RACED. As soon as they'd gotten away from the center of town, the man had pulled over and made her drive. She couldn't make out who he might be or what he wanted, but he knew to stay far enough away from her. If he didn't come close, she couldn't readily get the weapon. If he came in close to her, she could disarm him. She hadn't done it in a long time but she was confident enough in her skills to take the chance. Because what other choice did she have?

But he stayed carefully back away from her as he made her move to the driver's seat. Once she had her hands on the wheel, she had to focus on driving while he kept his weapon on Warrick. She willed Warrick to wake, at least to move so she'd know he was okay.

"Where are we going?" She tried asking the same question she'd asked moments before. Other than spitting out directions at her from time-to-time, the man hadn't spoken.

She cleared her throat and tried again, shooting for calm. "Can you tell me why you're doing this? What you want from us?" She glanced in the rearview mirror, hoping to see Warrick was still breathing. See some movement. Something.

He lay eerily still.

"Because it has to be different this time. It has to end." She almost jumped when the man spoke, but his words brought her no closer to understanding.

"I let you down before, Vicki. I know that. I won't do it this time." He was pleading with her.

Sara held her breath. He thought she was Vicki? Did he mean Warrick's wife? Why would he think she was Warrick's wife?

"I—" she started to speak then stopped. She didn't know if it was better to tell the man she wasn't Vicki or to go along with him. She didn't know what to do. Would it send him further over the edge if she convinced him she wasn't Vicki?

Then it hit her. *William Tyvek.*

The man had to be William Tyvek. She glanced over. She'd only ever seen pictures of the man, but he'd had gray hair in all of them. Could this be Tyvek?

A groan from the back seat drew Tyvek's attention and Sara checked the rearview mirror again. At least Warrick had made some noise. That had to be good. She hoped

"Get off here," Tyvek said as he scowled at Warrick in the backseat. "We have to get him to the house before he wakes up. You have to see him for what he really is this time. You need to see the devil and learn not to chase him and his temptations this time, Vicki. It's the only way."

Sara choked on the ball of bile in her throat as his words played in her head. *The only way.* For three such innocent words, they seemed entirely too ominous to her.

CHAPTER 37

JARROD RUBBED at the back of his neck. The feeling of ants biting at his skin back there wouldn't go away. He knew what that meant.

"Spidey senses goin' a little nutty, huh?" Cal asked.

"Yeah."

"Mine, too, brother." They'd gotten all the information they could from Darla and Buddy, before approaching their captain. Captain Calhoun hadn't been impressed. A strange look and dropped coffees wasn't enough for him to roll out the cavalry. Jarrod understood, but it didn't mean he could walk away from this.

Cal leaned closer to Jarrod. "The Captain said we couldn't waste resources looking for Warrick or Sara until we had evidence they were actually in trouble. Just because we can't check traffic cams or put out a BOLO doesn't mean we can't check out a few places on our own."

"Where? I doubt Tyvek would go to his house. It's been sealed up. In the past, his focus has been on Staunton. We can check the old Simms property again. See if he went back there." The doubt in Jarrod's voice said he didn't genuinely believe they'd be there.

"Hang on." Cal clicked keys while Jarrod waited. "Warrick's family owns properties around the world, but nothing close by."

Jarrod looked at his partner. He didn't have any ideas to offer and the frustration only pissed him off more.

"Let me check one more thing." Cal worked on the computer while Jarrod waited somewhat impatiently. Minutes later, Cal was frowning.

"What?"

"When we didn't find Tyvek in the apartment the Balls had put him up in, I checked to see if they owned other property anywhere in town that they might have put him up in. They have their house, but they also own a few rental properties, aside from the apartment building he'd been in. Could he be using one of those?"

"It's worth a look," Jarrod stood as Cal printed out a list of addresses. "How many are there?"

"Three."

"Let's hit those first. See what we find." Jarrod rubbed the back of his neck again. He wished instead of ant bites, he'd get clear instructions. They could sure as hell use it right now.

CHAPTER 38

JARROD AND CAL pulled up to the Staunton estate once again, ringing the buzzer at the front gates.

"Yes?" Came the female voice through the intercom.

"Detectives Harmon and Rylan from the New Haven Police Department. We need to see Mrs. Staunton."

"I'm sorry, she's not available."

"She needs to make herself available. Now." Jarrod practically growled into the little box. "Tell her it's about her son. We believe William Tyvek might have him." He wasn't above scaring the crap out of the woman to get results at this point.

Tyvek had proven he was dangerous. There was no telling what he might do if he did have Warrick and Sara. They'd been to both their residences and gotten no answer at either.

"Just a moment."

"You have to be shitting me," Cal grumbled.

Seconds later, they heard the mechanical sound of the gate clicking and the wrought iron swung open to let Jarrod pull up the drive.

He was surprised to see Warrick's mother waiting for them in the front entranceway. He'd been expecting to have to go through the formalities she seemed to favor of being shown to a room so she could make her entrance.

"Gentlemen," she said with a nod and turned to walk into the sitting room to her left.

Jarrod didn't waste time after following her in.

"We believe Tyvek has Warrick Staunton and his girlfriend."

"His girlfriend?" She seemed taken aback and Jarrod guessed Warrick didn't share much with his mother. He couldn't picture them having weekly phone calls or anything.

"Sara Blackburn."

She raised her brows but didn't comment on Sara or her relationship to Warrick. "I'm not sure how I can help. As I told you before, I don't know anything about Tyvek's whereabouts."

"And I think you were holding back on us." Jarrod wasn't going to pussyfoot around.

"We've been doing this a long time, ma'am," Cal said. "We know when we're not getting the full story."

"Nothing I can tell you will help," she snapped.

"Let us decide that. Tell us what you were holding back on last time we talked."

She shocked the hell out of Jarrod when she actually looked embarrassed. "It has nothing to do with what's going on. It's in the past."

Realization dawned. "You were having an affair with William Tyvek, weren't you?"

Anna Staunton sniffed as though the idea were distasteful or maybe it was just that talking about it was distasteful. "No. It ended years ago. William was a widower and my husband and I had," she paused, "certain agree-ments." A little shrug of her shoulders explained the rest.

"When was this?"

"Years ago. When Warrick was in high school."

Jarrod frowned as he thought back to what Carrie had told him about Warrick and Vicki. "Warrick was dating Vicki in high school, wasn't he?"

She raised her chin. "Yes."

Jarrod could see the look of shock on Cal's face and had a feeling he wasn't hiding his opinion much better. But he didn't care. "Did Warrick know?"

"No. We were discreet."

"You need to tell us now if you know anything about where Tyvek might be hiding. We know the Balls were hiding him, but they've been arrested and we raided the apartment they'd put him in." Jarrod had already had uniforms check the building in case Tyvek had taken Warrick and Sara back there. He hadn't and there'd been no sign he'd been back.

Her eyes went wide at the news. They'd kept the arrest of the Balls quiet and this confirmed it hadn't gotten out. If it had, she'd have known. He watched as she seemed to deflate a little. The woman didn't strike him as someone who had a lot of empathy for others but apparently, there was something there.

"I'm sorry, detectives. I really don't know how to help you. I'm not in contact with Tyvek. I don't have the slightest idea where he is or where he would take them."

Her voice shook in the smallest hint of her concern for her son, and unfortunately, Jarrod had a feeling she was telling the truth this time. They'd hit another dead end.

CHAPTER 39

SARA DIDN'T RECOGNIZE the house Tyvek directed her to, but she could take a few guesses. Something told her it wouldn't be Tyvek's own house. That had likely been seized by the police last month. It was possible the house was the one Warrick had sold, but wouldn't the new owners be here?

No. A dumpster. Sara took in her surroundings. There was a dumpster and the evidence of work being done on the house. But where were all the workmen? Or the neighbors? Surely someone would see them here and call the police?

Warrick was beginning to move in the backseat. Sara reached for him.

"Sorry, kitten. Can't let you do that." Tyvek pointed the gun her way, but still kept it far enough away from her that she couldn't move in close enough to disarm him. If he'd just reach out toward her with it, or let her get closer to him, she could stop all of this.

Sara shot another look at Warrick, whose eyes now focused on her with renewed sharpness, as though he was coming around and taking stock.

"Get out of the car, kitten."

Sara saw Warrick's slight nod. She opened the car door and stepped out. She would only have seconds while Tyvek got out of the car. She put her hands behind her back and twisted one of the fingers on her prosthesis, wrenching it.

Not enough pressure.

Tyvek got out, moving toward the back of the car. He held the gun on her but his focus was on Warrick. She braced the pointer finger of her prosthesis against her hip, and twisted again. The pressure on her stump sent pain shooting through her arm, but she ignored it. The finger gave way. She moved her hand behind her back again, twisting the finger free of the wires that still held it to the hand.

Tyvek called out to Warrick. "Your turn, Mr. Big Shot. Get out of the car."

Sara felt like she was watching some bizarre family sitcom where the father-in-law hated the son-in-law so much he was holding him at gun point. She wondered if Tyvek had called Warrick Mr. Big Shot at Thanksgiving dinners, then almost laughed at the strangeness of her thoughts in the face of a weapon. What the hell was wrong with her?

Warrick unfolded himself from the car, stumbling a bit as his legs moved to take his weight. His hands were bound behind his back, but his gaze locked onto Tyvek and he stood up straight.

"Let her go, Tyvek."

"I can't do that. I can't let her leave me again."

Warrick glanced from Sara to Tyvek and opened his mouth, but Sara jumped in before he could speak.

"I'm not leaving again, I promise." As she said it, Sara thought of Buddy who'd had the same concerns. She hoped

Tyvek was as easy to convince of that as Buddy was, but she wasn't going to hold her breath on that. For now, she was hoping to lull him into letting her closer.

Warrick didn't argue with her as Tyvek motioned toward the side of the house. "Move. We're going to the rose garden."

* * *

Warrick put himself between Sara and Tyvek as they walked around the corner of his old home. The house was set far back with a yard that stretched out in a yawning expanse on either side and a wooded double lot at the back. Stone walls contributed to the isolation of the space, something he'd once valued for its privacy, but now cursed as he thought about the gun at his back. He knew the new owners planned several months of renovations, leaving very little chance they'd discover what was happening at the moment.

He carefully flexed his fingers, ignoring the sharp pains as the feeling came back into his fingertips. He needed to be ready to move the second he could figure out a way to get his arms free. There was no way in hell he would let Sara down the way he'd let Vicki down.

They got out to Vicki's rose garden with its ceramic benches and the circular pattern of roses and pathways.

"Keep going. All the way to the center." Tyvek spoke gently, and Warrick had a feeling the man was talking to Sara now. Of course, he seemed to think Sara was Vicki, which might be a good thing. If Warrick couldn't get loose, he could at least convince Tyvek to let Sara go safely.

Sara looked back at Warrick and he murmured directions to her. "Right...left...left."

They came to the center of the maze and Warrick turned to face Tyvek.

"Let her go, William. You've got me, but it's time to let Vicki go. We don't want her to get hurt."

The sneer that crossed Tyvek's face gave Warrick his answer before Tyvek spoke. "Now you want to put Vicki's well-being first? That's rich, even coming from you." Tyvek turned to Sara. "Have a seat dear." He gestured toward one of the two ceramic benches. Only on this one, he'd laid a fleece blanket out for Sara to sit on.

Sara raised her hands up slightly. "I'd rather sit with my husband."

"He's not your husband anymore." Tyvek's sudden outburst made her jump slightly, but she kept her gaze steady and Warrick's gut clenched. Even if he could talk Tyvek into letting her go, he realized Sara wouldn't leave. She would try to stay and fight. That's who she was. God, he prayed he wasn't going to get her killed. "Till death do us part, Vicki. That's all you gave to him."

Sara rushed to Warrick and wrapped her arms around him, laying her head on his chest. The move startled Warrick, but he felt her press something small into his hands. He recognized the feel of it with a start. It was one of the fingers from her prosthetic hand. And at the end of it, a sharp gear stuck out about a quarter of an inch. She was giving him a way to cut the ropes at his wrists.

She was incredible. Even in the face of danger, she was thinking. She hadn't frozen or panicked.

Tyvek's voice turned achingly soft. "You gave him till death and he took it. He took a lifetime from you. Can't you see I want it to be different this time?"

Sara pulled away from Warrick and sat on the bench.

"Now, you." Tyvek gestured to the other bench. "You sit there."

Warrick lowered himself onto the other bench. "No blanket for me?"

Tyvek didn't bother with an answer. He turned to a bag on the ground and unzipped it. Warrick didn't wait to see what was in the bag. He worked his fingers back and forth over the rope with the gear Sara had given him, ignoring the way it cut into his fingers as he moved. He needed his hands free. He needed to get Sara away from Tyvek.

CHAPTER 40

SARA WATCHED as Tyvek dug through the bag he'd stashed in the bushes. When he brought out lighter fluid, she had to fight not to spring out of her seat and attack. She cut her eyes toward Warrick. He was managing to stay very still, but she could see the muscles in his arms flexing as he moved. She only hoped that meant the worm gear she gave him was working, that he could cut through the ropes with it. She kept her hands by her sides, hoping Tyvek wouldn't see her destroyed prosthesis.

She and Warrick locked eyes as she prayed over and over that he would break through the bindings. Tyvek knelt not far from her. He held the gun, but his focus was split now. He pulled two more cans of lighter fluid from the bag. That's when Sara realized many of the shrubs had been stripped. Of course, they were bare of leaves and flowers for the winter, but Tyvek had hacked away at them and a pile of branches lay next to the bench Warrick sat on.

Tyvek had begun to talk, but the words were hard to make out. He was ranting to himself, and Sara understood what mental health experts meant when they talked about a psychotic break. He appeared to be exactly that: broken.

"William," Warrick said, his voice steady. "Vicki always loved these roses. Don't do this here."

Tyvek stilled for a moment and Sara held her breath. Warrick had talked about Vicki in the past tense.

"I still do," she said quickly. "I love this rose garden. Warrick is right. Don't do this here."

Tyvek shook his head and looked up at her, bone deep sorrow etched on his features. "I should have done better by you. I was too concerned about what people would think. Not this time, though. This time, we're going to do this together and then you'll see, things will be better when he's gone."

Sara's stomach twisted and she thought she might be sick. She knew in Tyvek's sick mind, Warrick was the root of his daughter's problems.

Tyvek froze.

Her hand. He'd seen her hand. He stepped toward her, then spun toward Warrick. Sara couldn't wait to see if Warrick had freed his hands.

Sara took a chance. It was now or never and she knew of one sure way to get Tyvek to turn back to her, to get his focus off Warrick. "Dad!"

Sara held her breath for a split second before remembering to breathe. As Tyvek turned, she struck, using the heel of her hand and driving straight up to his nose. Contrary to urban legend, it wouldn't send the cartilage into his brain and kill him. But it would hurt like a mother and make his eyes water, giving her a few seconds' advantage.

The gun fell from Tyvek's hand and Sara dove for it, but he was on her almost instantly. Her right hand was pinned beneath her. With her prosthesis broken, she wasn't able to grab the weapon with her left hand, but she could shove it out of the way. She hit at it, sending it under the shrubs.

"Vicki," Tyvek choked out in a guttural sob. He looked at her as though he couldn't believe she'd hurt him, but Sara didn't feel anything for the man. He was a killer, and she wouldn't let him kill Warrick in some crazed revenge plot for his daughter.

She shoved hard at Tyvek with the elbow of her left arm, flipping over to her hands and knees. She scrambled to look for a weapon. Something. Anything. Her eyes scanned the area and she finally dove for the gun she'd only moments before shoved out of the way.

She felt Tyvek's hand clamp down on her ankle and she pitched forward, her head hitting the concrete bench.

Then Warrick was up and moving. His hands were free as he charged at Tyvek, tackling him. The two men flew over Sara and hit the ground. The sound of grunts and flesh hitting flesh rent the air.

CHAPTER 41

JARROD LIFTED his phone to his ear as Cal drove them to the last of the three properties owned by the Balls. So far, they'd found nothing of note happening at either of the properties. Jarrod had touched base with Warrick's assistant again. There was no sign of Warrick or Sara at the office yet and she hadn't heard from either of them.

"Chad?" Jarrod said when his friend answered the phone. "Are you at the office?" His friend Chad worked at Sutton Capital and was close with one of the best hackers in the country, a woman who also worked at Sutton.

"Yeah, what's up?" Jarrod summarized what was going on quickly. "Is Samantha there? I'm wondering if there's anything she can do to help us." He glanced at Cal. "Anything that maybe, we uh, can't do."

He was doing all he could to avoid flat-out asking Samantha to break the law, but he knew chad would get it. Their hands were tied and William Tyvek was a dangerous man. They needed to bring him in before he hurt anyone else.

"Hang on."

A Minute later he could hear Chad talking. In typical Chad fashion, he didn't bother with expansive explanations. He cut straight to the point. "William Tyvek might have Sara. Jarrod wants to know if you can track her somehow?"

Jarrod was expecting some mystical hacker solution. It wasn't what he got. "Jarrod," Chad said into the phone. "Samantha and Sara have the Find My Friend app. She's pulling it up now."

Jarrod knew the address as soon as Chad relayed it. Sara was at Warrick Staunton's old house.

"We'll keep you posted, Chad." He said, hanging up. He hit the dashboard to turn on the lights. "They're at Warrick Staunton's old house."

As Cal hit the gas and turned them onto the highway, Jarrod called into the Captain to see about getting backup. Hopefully he could convince the captain that she wouldn't be there unless she was in trouble.

CHAPTER 42

JONATHAN PACED THE CONFERENCE ROOM. He didn't know if his heart could take a whole lot more of this. Warrick was like a son to him and they'd only just gotten back to the point where he truly believed Warrick had forgiven him for his part in Tyvek's plan.

He had driven out to Warrick's townhouse before coming here. At the moment, he was waiting for a call-back from the car company. He was trying to convince them to track Warrick's car and give him the location, but of course, they were fighting it. He'd wasted time screaming at them and was now waiting for a call from one of the supervisors. The police hadn't been able to help.

Detective Harmon and his partner seemed to believe Warrick and Sara were in trouble, but their captain wasn't willing to back them until they had some evidence of that.

Charlotte entered the room, looking as concerned as he did. "I talked to one of Sara's friends at Sutton. The detectives just called there and one of the women had an app on her phone that located Sara. They're out at Warrick's old house."

"Would Warrick have any reason to be out there? Maybe this is all just a false alarm. He and Sara could have run out there for some reason and they just aren't answering the phone."

Charlotte was shaking her head before he finished. "The new owners have closed on the house. The sale's gone through and I'd know if any complications or issues had turned up. I can't imagine they'd have a reason to be there."

Jonathan's chest tightened as the small bit of hope he'd begun to grasp at fell away. He knew how reliable Charlotte was. She was on top of every little detail of Warrick's life. If something had happened at the house, Charlotte would know about it.

"Let's go," Jonathan said. "I'll drive."

Charlotte nodded and followed him out.

Jonathan had almost lost Warrick once with his betrayal and he'd been damned lucky to build back some of the trust they'd once had. He couldn't lose him now. He just couldn't.

CHAPTER 43

WARRICK COULD SEE that Sara had gone still. Too still. Her eyes were open, but she didn't seem to be seeing anything. He couldn't let this happen. Fuck, he just couldn't let this happen.

He realized his limbs weren't responding as quickly as they should be. Whatever drug Tyvek had given him, it was still in his system and was messing with him enough to even out this fight a little.

An elbow caught him in the face and he grunted and rolled. Tyvek reached for the lighter fluid, not seeming to care if he soaked himself as he drenched Warrick's chest with it. Warrick coughed as the fumes hit him, as the fluid splashed onto his face.

If Tyvek lit them both up, Sara would get caught in the fire quickly with no one to move her and no way to move herself.

Warrick reached around him, feeling for a rock, a branch, anything. His hand closed on one of the branches Tyvek had piled up. It wasn't big enough to knock Tyvek out. Warrick brought it up and aimed for Tyvek's eye, plunging as hard as he could.

The sound that came from Tyvek was guttural, a wounded animal. Warrick shoved, pushing Tyvek to the side.

Sara. He had to get to her. He could see her pushing to her knees, but she was unsteady and blood ran down the side of her face.

He reached her as he saw Tyvek grab the bag he'd been rifling through earlier. The eye Warrick had hit was closed, swollen and angry, but the other eye made one thing clear. Tyvek was beyond reason. The madness had taken hold of him. The transformation from man to monster couldn't be stopped.

Tyvek pulled out a lighter. Warrick grabbed Sara up in his arms and ran with her.

He hadn't heard sirens, but he saw Jarrod and his partner come around the side of the house as the same time that flames went up behind him.

CHAPTER 44

WARRICK FELT something click into place when Jonathan and Charlotte pulled up to the house. Things had been so off for him for so long. Since long before Vicki died. And they'd spiraled down from there. But Sara was safe. He'd gotten her away from Tyvek. Tyvek was dead. They hadn't been able to save him, and horrible as it was to say, Warrick felt nothing for the man. He prayed Vicki and their baby were at peace, but he couldn't care less if William Tyvek rotted in hell for all he'd done.

He looked at Jonathan and Charlotte as they ran up and smiled, but he didn't leave Sara's side as she lay on the gurney.

"Oh thank God, Warrick," Jonathan said and Charlotte came around to Warrick's side and pulled him into a tight hug.

"Don't you ever scare me like that again." Her words were quiet but strong and he had a feeling he'd be hearing more from her on the topic later. She'd probably bullet point it in a presentation for him.

He pulled back when she let go and smiled at her. "I'm sorry."

"Sara," Jonathan said.

"I'm okay," she said, but Warrick didn't like the way she sounded. He was used to strength where she was concerned.

Jonathan and Charlotte stepped back as the EMTs began to load Sara's gurney into the waiting ambulance, but Warrick didn't budge. No way he was leaving her side.

He held her hand, climbing in next to her. They wanted him on a stretcher of his own, but he'd already refused. He wanted to stay with Sara until they were sure her head injury wasn't worse than it was.

He was taking some comfort in the fact they weren't racing to the hospital with sirens blaring. On the other hand, part of him wanted to scream at them to hit the sirens and the gas and get her to a doctor. That, or climb up front and take care of it himself. He counted it as a small miracle he was controlling himself.

As the EMTs checked Sara's eyes, Warrick looked down at the mangled remnants of her prosthetic hand. He shouldn't be surprised she'd come up with a way for him to cut the ropes Tyvek had bound him with. That was who Sara was. Lucky for her, they had a pretty big stash of the bionic hands in her signature color back at Simms II.

He pressed the release for the prosthesis, relaxing the pressure that held it to her arm. She tried to object as he pulled it off but the EMT had put an oxygen mask over her mouth and nose.

"Shh, Sara, let me get it off. I want to check your arm." She'd have to trust him with this eventually. He held still and watched her eyes, waiting for her to assent.

She gave a small nod, and he removed the sleeve

covering her arm. There was some swelling and bruising already forming where she'd wrenched the prosthesis.

"Do you have something for this?" He asked the EMT but they were ahead of him. They'd broken out an ice pack and moved to take Sara's arm from him. "I'll hold it," he said, laying the ice pack in his lap and placing her arm on the towel they gave him. He wrapped the ice pack around to the other side, being sure to keep the towel between her skin and the ice, then looked up.

Her eyes held his and his heart kicked over at what he saw there. She trusted him. It was clear as day on her face.

"I love you," he mouthed. It was hardly romantic in the back of the ambulance, but he'd do the romance thing later. Right now, he just needed her to know.

EPILOGUE

A MONTH LATER, Warrick watched as Sara cut the ribbon on Simms II. The manufacturing facility was in full swing and she was working with a few of her friends on a prosthesis design for leg amputees. She had some ideas for over-the-knee amputees, hoping to cut down on the pain they felt when they connected a prosthesis close to the hip. Much to Jack Sutton's dismay, Sara had left Sutton Capital and was now working full time on the development side of things at Simms. She and Jonathan had a blast discussing ideas, even though they both worked on very different projects.

Cameras flashed and the employees that made up most of the group standing around them cheered. This symbolized a turning point for Simms Pharmaceutical. Sales in the pharmaceutical side of things had been ticking back up, and they'd soon need to hire more people. Warrick couldn't believe he'd been looking at laying people off months before.

Hell, for that matter, months ago he was alone with an empty shell of an existence. He grinned at the melodramatic thought. It wasn't like him, but he couldn't help it. His life couldn't be more full with Sara in it. Getting to sleep with her in his arms at night, waking up to her sleepy-eyed smile, having all of her instead of just a piece—it was... everything. Everything.

He was particularly fond of waking her up by loving her. Her eyes would flutter awake to his kisses and she'd smile and reach for him. He never tired of hearing her whisper his name in that moment of recognition when she realized what he was doing.

There were a lot of things he'd never tire of with Sara. Like the way she challenged him. And the way she always needed to have a project to work on, some problem to solve. How she could make him laugh easily and often. How she cared for her friends. How fiercely she loved.

He must have ended up with the kind of stupid smile he'd been told he wore when he was thinking about Sara. His mother touched his arm. "Don't drool over her in public, son. It's unbecoming." Her words weren't harsh or truly reprimanding. She'd softened considerably and had told him on more than one occasion she liked Sara. She said Sara had "gumption," and he'd be hard pressed to disagree. She did have that, and more.

"I'm having Jonathan take me home." Warrick's mother said. She patted him on the arm. She hadn't turned into a loving, doting mother or anything that drastic. But she'd shown up at the hospital and dinners at her house now included Sara and a lot less formality. They ate on everyday dishes and didn't have staff standing over their shoulders the entire time.

He smiled at her. "I'm glad you came." It was the truth. He'd wanted her to see that their family's legacy was going to make it.

She looked around at the buildings and the people, and nodded. "You did very well, Warrick. You did quite well."

He couldn't hold back a smile as he kissed her cheek.

Sara and Jack Sutton walked up as Jonathan and Warrick's mother walked away. Warrick slipped his arm around Sara. That little feeling of all being right in the world came whenever he held her.

"Can I talk you two into grabbing lunch before you head back to the office?" Jack asked.

"Sorry, Jack," Warrick said. "We have plans." He squeezed Sara and smiled down at her.

"We do?" Sara asked, looking up at him, her mouth forming an O.

"We do." He liked the way she scowled at him.

He had plans for tonight that would, he hoped, call for another celebration. Plans for Sara and a ring and a question he'd been dying to ask her for weeks. He planned to surprise her with a drive to New Hampshire as soon as they were finished here. He wanted to show her the cabin he'd bought and spend the weekend convincing her to marry him.

She'd stopped kicking him out at night, and it hadn't taken him long to realize waking up wrapped around Sara was something he wanted. Something he never wanted to end. He loved her with all his heart.

That first time she'd told him she loved him when they'd gotten home from the hospital, his world had felt like it had been righted. Like everything had been off and she'd set it right again.

He also knew she'd come to trust him. She didn't hide it from him when she was in pain. She took her prosthesis off in front of him now and didn't flinch if her arm brushed him. She didn't try to pull away if he took both her arms in his hands, like he did now. He wrapped her arms around his back and smiled at her as Jack shook his head with a smile and turned away.

"We're headed to New Hampshire for the weekend."

She quirked a brow. "Oh yeah? A cabin? Don't tell me we're relocating to a cabin in the woods. I'm not sure I'm cut out to live with no amenities."

He loved the way she talked about them as if there was no doubt they'd do this together. He thought about his uncle's question. *Is something calling to you?*

For a long time, the answer had been no. That had changed. Sara was calling to him. "No, just the weekend. I promise to have you back by Monday. Maybe Tuesday at the latest."

She grinned and pressed herself to him. "My boss will be mad if I miss work."

His grin was just as wide. "I'll have a talk with him."

Do you want to see Cal's story? Come on over to the Sutton Capital On the Line Series and continue the stories of the men you've come to love! Pure Vengeance is the first in the Sutton Capital On the Line Series: http://loriryanromance.com/book/pure-vengeance

ABOUT THE AUTHOR

Lori Ryan is a NY Times and USA Today bestselling author who writes romantic suspense, contemporary romance, and sports romance. She lives with an extremely understanding husband, three wonderful children, and two mostly-behaved dogs in Austin, Texas. It's a bit of a zoo, but she wouldn't change a thing.

Lori published her first novel in April of 2013 and hasn't looked back since then. She loves to connect with her readers.

For new release info and bonus content, join her newsletter at http://loriryanromance.com/lets-keep-touch/

Follow her on Facebook at
https://www.facebook.com/loriryanromance/
or Twitter at https://twitter.com/Loriryanauthor
or Instagram at
https://www.instagram.com/loriryanauthor/